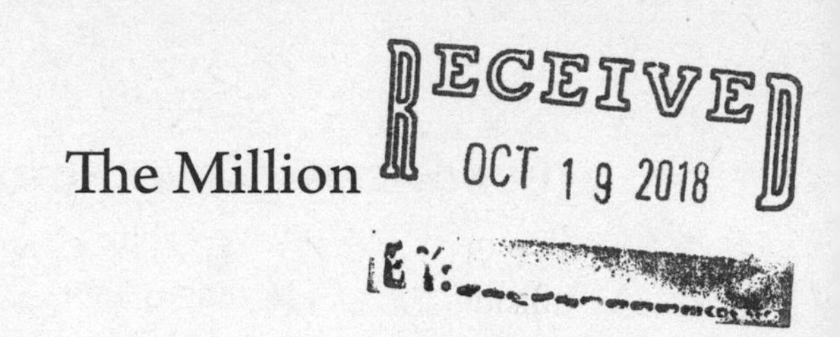

The Million

TOR BOOKS BY KARL SCHROEDER

Lady of Mazes
Permanence
Ventus
Sun of Suns
Queen of Candesce
Pirate Sun
The Sunless Countries
Ashes of Candesce
Lockstep

THE MILLION

KARL SCHROEDER

A TOM DOHERTY ASSOCIATES BOOK

NEW YORK

This is a work of fiction. All of the characters, organizations, and events portrayed in this novella are either products of the author's imagination or are used fictitiously.

THE MILLION

Cover illustration by Jan Weßbecher
Cover design by Jamie Stafford-Hill

Edited by Jonathan Strahan

A Tor.com Book
Published by Tom Doherty Associates
175 Fifth Avenue
New York, NY 10010

www.tor.com

ISBN 978-1-250-18541-9 (ebook)
ISBN 978-1-250-18542-6 (trade paperback)

First Edition: August 2018

For Paige. Not everything's a dystopia.

The Million

Gavin Penn-of-Chaffee smacked his brother's shoulder. "And what'll you do if they mob you?"

"Focus on one at a time," said Bernard through clenched teeth.

"And if somebody moves to cut you out of the pack?"

"Signal Dad."

"And if you have the sudden urge to hit somebody upside the head?"

"Retreat."

"Where?"

"Here."

Gavin scowled and gave his brother a critical once-over. "Okay, you're all set. Knock 'em dead."

"Don't say that if you don't mean it," warned Bernie. He took a deep breath, stepped up to the big pair of intricately carved, powder blue doors, and signaled the bots on either side to open them. Bernie stepped through the doorway into light and noise, and Gavin stepped back into the shadows. The doors swung shut, and Gavin's shoulders slumped.

Now for the hard part.

He walked through the pitch-dark sitting room at speed; though he rarely came down here, he knew exactly where every table and chair was. When he opened the door at the far end, it was to the exact same sight that had met him through the ones that Bernie had used. The vast ballroom Gavin strode into was packed with men in tuxedos and women wearing all manner of gowns, dresses, and visual confections. They were chatting, eating snacks off the trays of passing bots, raising glasses to this or that proposition, and, way too often, leaning together to eye Bernie and mutter as he passed by. They could have been holographic projections from the real ballroom, but they weren't; like the rest of the Million, Gavin had been raised to think of digital simulation as uncouth. Instead, this was a real double to the other room, and the "people" in it were fakes: bots made to look like the human guests visiting the Chaffee estate.

The one difference was that there were floor-to-ceiling windows in that other room, whereas here, hidden in the heart of the main building, the walls were blank.

Gavin watched the fake that was imitating his brother long enough to be sure that he wasn't about to bolt in terror. The bot not only looked like Bernie, it mimicked his expressions down to the finest detail, and repeated in his voice what he'd said in the other room. All looked good so far: he'd started a conversation with that girl in the lemon-yellow dress. Seeing this, Gavin turned away and closed his eyes.

Conversations, music, the tinkling of glasses, and the swish of skirts along the floor washed over him like a calming sea. Light laughter sang from his left, and he smiled; a dance started up, and he listened to the music echoing off the walls and the squeak of new shoes on the parquet floor. He tried to forget that this was Bernie's party and not his. He tried to imagine all these people gathering here to celebrate *him*.

But no, that was too much. He had no idea what such a moment would feel like.

There were more people at the Chaffee estate tonight than Gavin had ever seen gathered in one place. On any given day he might wander outside and face a vista of rolling hills and grasslands that never changed. Buffalo came by, sometimes wolves. Unless you owned a city, say, Paris or New York, this was all any of the Million normally saw. If he was bored, Gavin could summon the powers of his personal economy to build things of interest—palaces, flocks of autonomous skywriting aircraft, dungeons with fake dragons in them, mechs that he and Bernie could battle. He could re-create some historical city on the grasslands of central North America, fill it with fakes, and live like the ancients did for a day or a week or until he lost interest. In that way, his had been an ordinary life.

He listened as two women greeted each other just behind him, and he pictured himself standing next to one of them, her fingers wrapped around his arm. He could open his eyes and entwine his arm in that of one of the fakes and pretend he was actually in that other room, actually among those people.

. . . And that would just be creepy, and sad, and wrong; spying on them this way was already a mistake. He should be in his own chambers, in his own wing of the house, curled up with a good book. The only reason he'd done this was to keep a brotherly eye on Bernie. But he had to let go sometime. Dejected, he walked to the door and raised his hand to dismiss the fakes.

Despite himself, he turned for one last look. There were quite a few young people in the crowd. What would it be like to walk among them? To talk to them? Bernie's guests were intimidating, all of them beautiful or handsome, perfectly dressed, and perfectly poised. Like most of the scions of the Million, these ones were intensely focused, serious, and cautious around their elders. They should be—all of human civilization rested on their shoulders. Each was doubtless determined to become the greatest composer, pilot, scientist, or philosopher of this generation. All knew that if there were only one million people alive in the whole world, then those million had a responsibility to be equal to all who had come before.

"Stop skulking about, Neal," snapped an older man's voice. "This is a party, not one of your hunts."

The speaker was an older man, his face eclipsed by the head of a youth who was turned away from Gavin. All Gavin could see of the pair was their shared shaggy hair and hulking shoulders. Then the younger one looked around and sneered at the crowd, and Gavin froze.

He knew that face.

Gavin had been eleven or twelve years old. There was a party—not like this one, much more relaxed and friendly sounding—and some of the neighbors had been there. As usual, Father had told Gavin to stay hidden, but he couldn't resist peeking around a doorjamb to see the guests with his own eyes. That's when one of the Makhav boys had spotted him.

It was just a meeting of the eyes, no words had been exchanged, yet Gavin would always remember that face. It was the only time in his entire life that he'd locked gazes with someone outside his own family.

Neal Makhav-of-Winter-Park had grown up, was in fact a young man now. That would make Gavin one, too, he supposed. Little good that it did him.

Neal's fake stepped away from the older one and said, "You're one to talk, Father. You're just here to laugh at the gimp, like everybody else!"

"Don't use such language," warned Neal's father. "You knew Bernie before the accident. He was a great kid."

Neal gave a contemptuous snort. "Yeah, but he zigged when he should have zagged. Getting that iron bar through the head scrambled his brains, so what's he good for now? Somebody should put him out of his misery."

You could strike a fake without consequences, but Gavin's father had always warned him never to do it. "You might get used to hitting them, and that would make you used to hitting people," he'd said. So Gavin kept his clenched fists at his sides. It was little consolation that Neal's father had stepped in front of his son and was glaring into his face.

"Don't you even *think* of trumping up some sort of duel with Bernard Chaffee," he hissed. His eyes widened as Neal glanced away. "You *were* thinking of it!"

"Come on, Father, it's not like I haven't put down wounded animals before. And look at this place! Six thousand square kilometers of land, and just the two of them to take care of it? Old man Chaffee's got no heir now, it's just a matter of time before he admits defeat. Should have done so before now. Everybody says so."

Neal's father crossed his arms and turned away. "The Chaffee lands are thriving. And Bernie's no idiot. The injury didn't affect his intellect, only his self-control." He shook his head. "I can't believe you'd consider such a thing."

"Don't get me wrong, I wouldn't have killed the guy. But this party is pathetic; it's a sham and it needs to be exposed. I mean, do they really think that one of those girls is going to take to him? . . . And anyway"—and here Neal looked everywhere but at his father's eyes—"I still say Bernie's had help running the place."

"This again? You swear you saw another boy here once and now you're convinced they're hiding a visitor on the property! That's ridiculous."

"I know what I saw," said Neal, and his fake turned its head and looked straight through Gavin.

The illusion was so startling that for a second Gavin was sure that Neal could really see him.

Oh, he did remember that night. After he and Neal Makhav locked eyes, Neal had kicked up a fuss, asking who the other boy in the house was, but by that time Gavin had hidden himself, and ordered his bots to do the same with any evidence that there was a third person there. Father had laughed and given the nosy boy a chance to search the whole place, just to prove there was nobody here. Neal had done so, much to the embarrassment of his father and uncle.

"—not a fit profession for a Makhav," Neal's father was saying. "It's not an honorable use of the hunting skills I gave you."

Neal snorted in contempt. "I knew you'd say something like that. But my mind is made up."

"This isn't the time or place for this," said his father. "We'll talk about it when we get home."

Neal Makhav took several steps away from his father, then turned and sent him an aloof look. "No, we won't, Father. You see, after we're done here, I'm not going home." He walked away.

Before he could follow Neal, another man stepped up to Neal's father. He was gray haired though still powerfully built, and here, too, the family resemblance was plain. Gavin had seen photos of Eli Makhav; Father made sure he knew about all the important players in the region. Eli was the brother of the Makhav clan's patriarch, and Father said it was really Eli who ran the household, childless though he was.

"Made up his mind, has he?" said Eli, as both men stared at Neal's retreating back.

"He'll come around. This thing about joining the auditors . . . it's just youthful restlessness," said Neal's father.

"I'm not so sure about that. And what's he up to now?" Neal was nudging one of the ballroom's marble statues (also faithfully reproduced in the room where Gavin stood) as if trying to make it fall off its pedestal.

Eli sighed and walked over to him. Gavin followed; he just had to hear this.

Eli came to a halt next to his nephew. Without looking at him, he said, "Break it and I'll crack your head wide open."

Neal looked startled, then guilty, and then began to slink away. Suddenly Eli's hand was clamped on his wrist.

"That goes double for Bernard Chaffee," he said. Neal pulled away but couldn't even get the older man's arm to quiver.

Eli let go, and Neal stepped back, snarling as he rubbed his bruised wrist. Then suddenly he laughed.

"I don't have to do anything, old man," he said. "Look!"

Eli turned, and Gavin turned, and so just managed to catch the moment when Bernie's hard-won self-control failed.

He'd clearly been trying to hold a conversation with one of the girls, but others had gathered around, perhaps reassured by his calmness. They were curious. Later, Gavin would forgive them for it, but now they pressed close, trying to hear, and Gavin could see it all become too much for Bernie. The unfamiliar people, the babble of voices and moving bodies, the pressure to be at his best, anxiety at meeting the girls . . . any of these could have pushed Bernard Chaffee over the edge, and right now they were all present at once. Father reminded him to keep Bernie's exposure to strangers short, but the problem was, Bernie always *seemed* fine, right up until that moment when he—

"No!" Bernie swung his drink and champagne sprayed those nearest him. "Get away, I can't, I don't wanna, I—"

"Aw, no, Bern," said Gavin. He took two steps toward his brother, but this wasn't really Bernie, just a robotic actor faithfully playing out a drama to which Gavin wasn't invited.

He ran out of the utility room and through the darkened lounge, and put his hand on the door to the real ballroom. He could hear Bernie's panicked voice through the thick wood of the door.

It wasn't too late. He knew what to do, the words to say to back Bernie off and settle him again. He knew how to do it. But he couldn't go in there.

If he did, everyone would learn that Martin Chaffee was harboring an illegal visitor. That wasn't necessarily a capital crime, but Father had always acted as if Gavin's case was different. There was some dire reason for his remaining hidden here—and that reason trumped all other considerations.

He let go of the knob but pressed his ear to the door.

"All right, Bernard, son," Father was saying in a soothing tone. Didn't he know that never worked? "Excuse us, everyone," he said in a louder tone. "It's all been a bit too much for Bernard, I'm afraid."

Don't talk about him like he's not there! Gavin raised his fists, and though he would never actually smack his—no, Bernie's—father alongside the head, Gavin made the gesture here in the safety of the darkness.

Bernard's not stupid, he's as smart as you are! That's why he's so frustrated.

You couldn't think your way around a brain injury. Gavin had seen Bernie try, many times. He knew perfectly well how he should be behaving; it was just that he literally didn't have it in him to do it.

Bernie was shouting now, and the guests were muttering. Gavin heard a flapping noise and pictured Father trying to keep Bernie's flailing fists down. He couldn't summon a bot to subdue his own son, that sort of thing just wasn't done. He was going to get hit.

Gavin threw open the door.

Everything was exactly as he'd pictured it would be. Bernie was bigger than Martin Chaffee, and he'd just gotten in a roundhouse blow that had sent Father reeling. Some of the guests stood in a semicircle, shocked by the scene, while others were making for the door.

"Wait, wait," Father shouted after them. "It's all right, he's just nervous."

"Can we help?" Two big-shouldered young men (more Makhavs, maybe?) stepped forward. They looked eager to tackle Bernie, but Eli Makhav moved surprisingly quickly, putting himself between them and Gavin's brother.

"This is a family matter," he grated. "Stand down."

Gavin spotted Neal Makhav. He was standing near one of the big glass doors that led outside, his arms crossed, a contemptuous smile on his face.

Nobody had seen Gavin yet, and when a face did turn his way, it was his father's. When he spotted Gavin, his eyes widened and his face flickered through a whole host of emotions—fury, shame, resignation. Right there, in one second, Gavin read the past sixteen years of Martin Chaffee's life. Then Father tilted his chin up in an unmistakable gesture: *Get back!*

Gavin stepped into the shadowed lounge and eased the door shut. Through the curtained windows off to the right, he could hear somebody laughing on the front lawn. It wasn't a nice laugh.

It took ten minutes for Bernie to calm down enough that Father could haul him out of the room. By that time most of the guests had left. Gavin heard his brother and father coming—a gathering storm of argument and thudding footsteps—and then the door burst open and Bernie stumbled into the lounge. He was disheveled and tearstained in the fan of light from the ballroom.

Martin Chaffee slumped against the door like a broken doll, his face empty of expression. Gavin went to him and said, "Go," pointing out the door. "Salvage what you can." The Makhavs were still here, along with some other stalwart friends who'd known Bernie since before the accident. They would help his father recover some of his shredded dignity.

Martin nodded wearily and left. Gavin turned to Bernie.

"It happened," Bernie said. He banged his fists against his temples, not softly. "Again, again, again. It's always going to happen, I can't stop it."

This was threatening to be a repeat of thousands of similar conversations. Gavin had tried as many ways of deflating Bernie's self-pity and none had worked. Suddenly weary of even trying, he barked a humorless laugh and said, "And why should you?"

Bernie blinked at him. "What?"

"Well, it's *their* problem if they can't deal with you." He threw a hand out to indicate the curtains and the grounds beyond, where aircars like confections of light were lifting off. "Would you really want to be friends with somebody who couldn't accept you for who you are?"

Bernie seemed at a loss as to how to answer that. Finally, he went to sit in an overstuffed leather armchair under a portrait of one of his ancestors. Douglas Penn-of-Chaffee seemed to glower disapprovingly at Bernie;

Gavin was convinced that Bernie was aware of this effect and sat there specifically to cause it.

He looked up at Gavin. "Then why do we try?"

Gavin crossed his arms. "Because your real friends are out there somewhere. They've gotta be. But we're not gonna find them if we don't look."

"Gotta be?" Bernie croaked contemptuously. "There's only a million people in the whole world. It took more than a billion before there could be a Picasso."

"It doesn't take genius to like you, Bernie."

"It takes something." Bernie wasn't looking at him anymore, and Gavin, embarrassed, went to the window to twitch back the curtain. Sometimes Bernie's intelligence startled even Gavin, and he'd known Bernie nearly his whole life. *It takes family,* he thought to himself—but that was useless because the Chaffees were not like the Makhavs. There were nearly a hundred Makhavs—fractious, quarreling, mutually suspicious though they might be. But here, there were only Martin Chaffee and his sons, one of whom wasn't supposed to exist, and one who didn't want to.

Neither of them spoke for a long time. All they had ever said to each other hung in the air between them. One of the things Bernie had said, and more than once, was, *"I should have died."* Gavin's answer to that was always the same: *"But then I'd be alone."* A thin argument, but sometimes it was all he had.

There was a polite knock on the door and a bot opened it. "The last of the guests have left, sirs," it said.

Gavin left the lounge, then looked back. Bernie hadn't moved. "Are you just going to sit in the dark?" he asked.

"Yes," Bernie said. There wasn't any anger or sullenness in the way he said it; his voice sounded almost like he was laughing. Gavin sighed and finally remembered the fakes in the other room. He practically ran back to the utility room to dismiss them before either Father or Bernie found them.

Back in the ballroom, Father was slumped in an armchair, swirling red wine in a crystal glass and pressing a cold rag against his cheekbone. Quite a bruise was developing around Martin Penn-of-Chaffee's left eye. Two bots hovered in the background, eager to provide assistance. He ignored them, but sent a glance at Gavin as he came to lean against the arm of a velvet-chased couch nearby.

Neither spoke, and a few minutes later Bernie emerged from the lounge. He, too, was subdued, but he walked up to his father and said, "I've been giving it some thought." He blew out a heavy sigh. "I think it's time for Plan B."

Their father closed his eyes, an expression of such pain that Gavin hopped up from his slouch. "What?" he said. "What's Plan B?"

Father and Bernie looked at each other, then both turned to gaze quietly at Gavin. The look on their faces was almost identical—eloquent and sad, but Gavin didn't know what it meant.

"Tell me," Gavin insisted.

"Not now," said Father. He glared at Bernie. "We'll talk about it in the morning. We're all a little too . . . ragged . . . right now."

Gavin looked from one to the other. "But what—"

"In the morning. That's an order," Martin said directly to Bernie. Bernie ducked his head and walked away.

"Go to bed, Gavin," said his father. Gavin shifted from one foot to the other, wondering whether he should press the issue. He was so weary, though, and so much had happened. Finally, he nodded just like Bernie had and stumbled off to his room, where images and snatches of conversation from the evening rolled around and around in his head for what seemed like hours, defying sleep.

• • •

"Master Gavin, you must wake up."

He jerked in surprise. The blankets slid off as he sat up. A bot stood at the foot of his bed. Its face was a stylized mask of porcelain. The room was lit only by the blue flashlight in the bot's raised left hand.

"What's wrong?"

"Your father requests your presence in the great room."

"W-what? What time is it?"

"Three a.m., sir."

"Lights." He grabbed the shorts and a shirt that another bot was holding out and paced quickly into the corridor, which lit up as he entered it. Gavin blinked and looked around; there were bots bustling everywhere, but he couldn't figure out what they were doing. He ran along the deep crimson carpet, past marble statues and tall stone urns, into the frescoed hall where he'd last seen his father.

Martin Chaffee might not have moved at all since Gavin had last seen him; he was slumped in the same armchair as before. But he wore a housecoat now and his hair was disheveled.

"Dad, what—?" Gavin thought he'd figured out what had happened, so he was surprised when he saw Bernie descending the stairs, a confused frown on his face.

A wash of guilt made Gavin turn his face away. He'd thought, *Has Bernie killed himself, or run off?*—and here none of it was true. He never gave Bernie the benefit of the doubt, always expected the worst from him. He had to stop doing that.

His father said, "We have visitors."

It took a few seconds for the words to register. Bernie and Gavin looked at each other, then their father. "What?" said Bernie.

"A bot just woke me," said Father. "An air force is approaching from the southeast. There are at least two hundred craft. They didn't answer our hails, so the house scrambled our own fighters. This is happening now."

An air force. Bernie stood frozen for a moment. Gavin shook his head, confused. Everybody had armies and air forces, or if you lived on the coast, a navy or two. Why not? They were fun toys. But war was a prearranged, family outing. This sounded like a sneak attack—something from ancient history.

As if responding to his motion, the lights suddenly went out.

The darkness was punctuated by the sounds of things falling throughout the house: crashes and bangs and tumbling and, just a couple of meters away, the crumpling thud of the nearest bot hitting the floor. Then bangs like sudden thunder rolled in from the distant windows.

Gavin saw his father's silhouette as Martin Chaffee leaped to his feet.

"Boys," he shouted. "Run!"

• • •

"But what—what just—" Gavin stood up, and he heard Bernie running to join him.

Their father's voice sounded from a meter away. "They've used a magnetic pulse weapon on us. Knocked out all our bots, at the very least."

"Who?"

He half saw, half felt Father move past him to where Bernie stood. "Bernard, he's defended you, in his own way, these past years. It's time for you to return the favor."

"Yes, Dad." Then Gavin felt Bernie's big hand clamp down on his shoulder, and he was being hauled out of the great room. Gavin shouted and pulled away, but Bernie's grip was unbreakable. "Dad!" Gavin shouted back. "Dad! What are you doing?"

"I'll be all right, son. I'm just going to talk to them. Wait in the caves for my all clear."

Bernie didn't steer around the invisible furniture or downed bots, just stepped over them or kicked them aside. Gavin wrestled himself free but couldn't decide what to do next. Bernie was crashing through the glass-ceilinged arboretum with its strangely silent fountains. Gavin took one last look down the corridor; Martin was lighting a lamp, his face suddenly drawn and old in its orange light. Gavin raced to catch up with his brother.

Bernie opened the back door and stopped so suddenly that Gavin ran into him. Off to the left, the sky was punctured by multiple flashes of light and rolling thunder. Nearer, the tearing sound of an aircraft echoed across the grounds, and past Bernie's shoulder, Gavin saw a small vessel slide by, not more than thirty meters up—a modest two-seater, from its lines.

Bernie tensed, then: "Now!" He raced for a grove of trees whose peninsula of green nearly reached the arboretum. On hot days it was convenient to use their shade to reach some of the outbuildings; only now, as he ran under them with his brother, did Gavin think that they might also have been planted to make it harder to see escaping people from the air.

Moonlight sketched the path under the trees. Gavin looked back during a brief pause when both he and Bernie were catching their breath halfway up the western hill.

The mansion and outbuildings of the Chaffee estate were the only man-made structures within hundreds of kilometers. Gavin had been up here at night many times and knew what he should see—but he wasn't seeing it. There were always windows lit in the mansion, yard lights and other illumination scattered for many hectares around. It was all black now, as if the encircling wilderness, so carefully renewed by the Chaffees for generations, had simply reached in and devoured the estate.

Dark silhouettes blocked the stars, dozens of them descending to the lawns and gardens, and as his eyes adjusted he could just make out human shapes—but they must be bots—fanning out around the house. Some of the shadowed forms were huge.

"Those're military," Bernie said, nodding at the hulking bots.

"They're here for *me?*" Gavin heard his voice squeak on the last word. But Bernie shook his head.

"The auditors wouldn't send soldier bots to pick up one visitor. Somethin' else is going on. Come on." He grabbed Gavin's arm again and hauled him farther up the slope.

The trees ended high up the hillside. At the top of this grassy ridge was a sudden drop of about five meters; there, the tilted, grass-covered table of rock they were running on exposed a softer underside. Caves were hollowed into it, just shallow things that didn't go back more than seven meters or so. They'd been kept a secret from all guests, and Bernie was making for them now.

When Gavin tried to follow him, Bernie turned and shoved him away. "Split up in the open, stupid," he said. Then he was off, running to the right. Gavin took the left.

He'd made it halfway to the top when the whole plan fell apart. Red running lights suddenly lofted above the ridge directly ahead of him. The little aircar they'd seen earlier wobbled, lurched forward, and began to descend.

Gavin spun on one foot and began to run back down the slope. A black shadow sailed right over him, kicking up grit and straw in its wake, and then the car was in front of him again. The message was clear: he was trapped. He turned anyway and bolted for the ridge, thinking of the caves. But the car swept insolently in between him and them.

He'd occasionally thought about what he would do if the auditors caught him. Now, as the aircar settled onto the very top of the ridge and its canopy swung back, he straightened his shoulders and walked right up to it.

"That's close enough." The rifle was aimed right at his chest. "What luck," said the aircar's only occupant. "I found the one that got away."

Shocked and confused, Gavin said nothing as his captor climbed out of the car. Then he looked past the lowering rifle, and without thinking said, "You're Neal Makhav."

With a hiss, Neal Makhav-of-Winter-Park raised the rifle and put his finger on the trigger. "Have you been spying on me? On us? How dare you even speak the name of one of the Million! You have no right to be here."

Cold fright told Gavin to run, but he knew he had only one defense now. He struggled to find his voice.

"You set the auditors on us."

Makhav made a noncommittal noise, tilting his head from side to side. "Okay, no. Wish I had. I knew you were here. Saw you once, years ago. But I didn't call *them* in tonight. Was awake when they overflew our land, heard Uncle talk to them on the radio. I knew you were here, I knew they must be coming for you at last. So I followed."

Gavin swallowed, keenly aware of the unwavering barrel of the rifle aimed at him. He had to keep Neal talking, keep his attention fixed.

"That's a lot of luggage in your car, there," he observed. "And no bots to pilot it for you. No escort either. Are you leaving home?"

Another hiss, and the rifle shook just a bit. Then Neal Makhav lowered it a centimeter and said, "It's none of your business! The auditors are here. I want to apply, I asked to, so I came to find 'em. And look what I did! They'll have to let me in after I caught you, won't they?" His lips curled into another contemptuous smile.

Gavin struggled to keep his voice steady. "Come on, then. Walk me down the hill like a proper bounty hunter, and I'm sure you'll get your reward."

Neal Makhav shook his head. "No. See, I thought about this. It's one thing to round up 'visitors.' Anybody could do that, and what are they gonna say? 'Thanks, kid. We'll take it from here.' Proves nothing. But to actually *kill* an illegal, now that . . ." He raised the rifle and aimed before Gavin could react.

Then Makhav wasn't there and his rifle was tumbling end over end down the hillside. As Gavin fell to his knees, he glimpsed Bernie and Makhav in midair over the ridge's five-meter drop. Makhav shouted in surprise and they disappeared.

Gavin's legs felt like jelly as he scrambled over to the aircar and laid his trembling hands on the rifle.

He was about to run to the lip of the ridge when he heard a shout from behind him. He turned, too shocked and fearful now to be surprised at the sight of someone emerging from the trees. The man wore the uniform of the Human Sustainability Task Force, and fanning out behind him were dozens of terrifying armored shapes—not willowy harvesters or the unobtrusive servant bots Gavin was used to, but huge, hulking iron apes, shambling, multilimbed, and bristling with weaponry.

Behind them, fire was thrusting and battering its way through the windows of the mansion—first on the ground floor, then the second, and the third.

A noise behind him, and Gavin turned again. Bernie climbed over the exposed stone lip of the ridge and stood up. His face was a mask of rage.

"Point the rifle at me," he snapped.

"W-what? Where's Makhav?"

"Point the damned rifle at me!" Bernie loomed forward, his hands like claws. "Makhav landed on his face. He's dead."

"Dead!"

"Point the damned—" Bernie snatched at the rifle and Gavin reflexively lifted it. "Aim it at me," Bernie ordered.

Gavin did as he was told, just as the auditor arrived.

"You can lower it now, son. He's not going anywhere." The man was elderly, like so many of the Million, but his strength and health were clear under the weathered skin of his bare arms and face.

He's not going anywhere? The bots had all kinds of weapons out, but they were aimed at Bernie, not Gavin. Suddenly realizing what all this looked like—what Bernie had done—Gavin lowered the rifle.

"Who're you?" the auditor asked.

"B-Bernard. Bernard Penn-of-Chaffee," said Gavin's brother. He was staring at Gavin wide-eyed, like he was trying to push him back by force of will alone.

"And you?" The auditor turned to Gavin.

"I-I'm—"

"Makhav," grated Bernie, "Neal Makhav-of-Winter-Park. You were at our party. You must have called 'em. You killed my brother!" And he wailed, and made as though to charge the whole group. Long habit made

Gavin drop the rifle and jump to stop him. That had always been his job, after all. This time, they were swarmed and pulled apart. Iron hands drove Bernie to his knees.

"My brother!" Bernie wailed again. "He's dead, you killed him!"

"What's he talking about?" asked the auditor.

Gavin stammered, then said, "Another one. He ran off the ridge when I landed."

One of the soldier bots released some little drones, like flying knives. They soared out over the ridge, shining little spotlights down. "One body, sir," said the soldier. "No visible wounds but a broken neck."

"My brother, my brother," Bernie moaned. Gavin stared at him in wonder.

Brain-damaged, not stupid. As Gavin watched his brother perform now, he felt a welcome welling of pride.

"This is all a little too easy," said the auditor. He looked Gavin up and down. "If you are who you say you are, you won't mind proving it." He led Gavin in the direction of the aircar.

"Y-yes, sir." Gavin locked eyes with Bernie, who gave an almost imperceptible shrug. Well, they'd tried.

He should just admit the lie now, but Gavin found himself stubbornly stepping up to the aircar as though it were his. He scanned its interior for any sign of bots, but Neal Makhav really had flown out here alone. His shoulders hunched as he saw the big monitor on the pilot's console.

The auditors wouldn't need a bot to confirm his lie. "Call in," instructed the auditor, nodding at the screen.

Gavin stared at the screen. He couldn't move, the thought of how this was going to go was just too overwhelming. "Well, what are you waiting for?" demanded the auditor.

As if from a distance, he watched himself climb into the cockpit and press the Home icon on the monitor. The screen displayed the word "Calling," and the seconds dragged. Outside, he could hear the military bots saying that the body's face was too mashed for immediate identification.

A square, tanned face flashed onto the screen. "Eli Makhav," said an impatient voice.

The auditor leaned in next to Gavin. "I'm sorry to disturb you so late at night, Mr. Makhav," he said formally. "I'm Thomas Jagand-of-Karelia, of the auditors. There's been an incident up in Chaffee and I just need to confirm something with you."

"Oh?" Eli Makhav's left eyebrow twitched upward slightly. His gravelly voice deepened a bit as he asked, "What kind of incident?"

"Martin Penn-of-Chaffee called us an hour ago saying that his son had gone berserk. He requested an intervention, as Bernard had taken control of some of the house bots and was sending them after his father. When we got here, Chaffee was dead."

Gavin bit back the shout that would have betrayed him. Instead, he went completely still.

"The Chaffee constitution forbids patricide, so we've taken the son into custody. But there's another young man who just arrived. He's claiming to be Neal Makhav, of your clan."

On the screen, Eli Makhav's gaze switched from the auditor to Gavin. His eyes narrowed.

"I went to find the auditors, like I said I was going to," Gavin said quickly. The whole idea that he could fool Eli Makhav into thinking he was Neal was ridiculous. His only chance was to try an entirely different tactic. He thought about what he'd heard Neal Makhav say earlier tonight. "Imagine my luck to find 'em coming here! A whole flight of Task Force units converging on Old Man Chaffee's place. Landed to find out what was going on, saw kind of a fight. Bernie was about to ambush the auditors, so I stepped in. You know I always said he deserved to be put down. They wouldn't let me do it, but—" Out of the corner of his eye he saw Karelia frown. "I caught him," Gavin finished, lifting his chin proudly. "You know me." But Eli Makhav's eyes had gone wide. Even Bernie was staring gape-mouthed. This was never going to work.

The one thing Gavin knew about Eli Makhav was that he intensely disliked his nephew. Reminding him just how murderous Neal was had been his only play, and surely it wouldn't work.

Eli Makhav's image was unmoving, as though the video feed had been replaced by a photo. Karelia growled impatiently and said, "All I need is for you to confirm to me that this one really is Neal Makhav-of-Winter-Park, of your family. As to rumors of a visitor . . . I'll ask you not to spread them any further, sir."

Eli Makhav looked back at Gavin. He was silent for a moment. Then: "What are you playing at, boy?"

Gavin glanced at Bernie, who had begun this desperate gambit. It must be killing him to keep his raging impulses in check. Gavin couldn't let him down. "I want to join the auditors. I left, I did what I said I would do, and I'm *never coming back*."

Makhav's eyes narrowed just slightly and something that might have been a smile played around the corners of his mouth. It was gone before Gavin could tell for sure.

"Tell me the truth. Did you kill this . . . this *visitor,* son?"

Gavin shook his head. "He fell off the ridge, sir."

Makhav sat there silently for a few seconds, then, in a musing tone, he said, "That was quite the knock-down, drag-out argument that young Neal had with his father when we got home. Things were said that can never be unsaid. It wouldn't surprise me if the two *never talked to each other again."* He was staring straight at Gavin.

"Yes, sir. I mean no, sir," said Gavin.

Eli Makhav returned his attention to Karelia. "He's Neal Makhav, all right. Though he's a tad dustier than usual."

"Very good!" Karelia beamed at the monitor. "Since he was the one who caught Bernard Chaffee, I'd say he's shown good presence of mind today. He'll be a fine addition to the auditors."

"I'm sure he will," said Makhav drily. "Don't you worry about any . . . rumors. I will accept whatever the official investigation says happened tonight. As to this one, he and his father may have had a falling-out, but I intend to keep a very close eye on him from now on." He shot Gavin a sharp look, then reached out, and the monitor went blank.

Gavin stared at the blank screen, half-aware that bots were stomping back and forth, spotlights were being aimed and lit, and the sky was filling with the dark war machines of the Millions' auditors. It was only when Karelia slapped the aircar's canopy that he started and looked up.

"Right!" said Karelia. "We've got details to take care of here." He stepped down from the cockpit.

Gavin stood up and met Bernie's eye again. "What are you going to do with him?" he asked, as levelly as he could manage.

"He'll be tried for the murder of his father," said Karelia. "Then we'll see.

"Set your course for Rochester," he told Gavin. "Ask for one of our airships there, it'll take you to Venice."

Gavin blinked and sat down in the cockpit. "What's in Venice?" he asked dumbly.

Karelia cocked his head and laughed. "Why, the school, at least this year's." With that, he turned and walked away.

Bernie formed his mouth into one word: *Go.* Gavin sobbed, then hauled the canopy closed, and the aircar whirred, rose, and turned east.

• • •

A ribbon of blood spiraled around Elana Devries's wrist. She hesitated at the curtained, beveled-glass doorway, the fingers of her other hand tracing the gold filigree that ran around the glass. Two bots dressed as footmen held the door handles, waiting. Baroque music drifted in on the air.

"Just wipe it off!" She was late, and she had to cross the salon without attracting attention. Well, that wasn't an option, the way she was dressed. The rough hunter's clothes were one thing. Sporting a big white bandage as well was bound to attract comment from her sister. Katharine Devries-of-Balashikha could smell blood—or impropriety, anyway. If she found a hair out of place on Elana's head, she would pounce.

"Give me a cotton wad." A bot cleaned up her arm and handed her a white puffball, which she pressed against the inside of her arm. Then she crossed both arms under her breasts, hoping that she would merely look cold, and launched herself into the salon.

Five couples were practicing a formal dance on the parquet floor. Elana hugged the wall and ducked behind the robot musicians, hoping that the others would be concentrating on their footwork. And she nearly made it.

"Elana!" Katharine's liquid laugh froze her in midstep. "Is that truly what you're wearing to my birthday party?"

The couples broke off their dance, and the bots stopped playing. Pinned like a butterfly by her sister's attention, Elana forced herself to turn and smile. "You've been partying for a week already, Kate. Surely I can have some time of my own?"

Katharine wore a crinoline, lace, and silk ball gown designed by Seyna Alagast-of-Nairobi. The bodice was a tangle of diamonds and platinum wire sprouting from the flower that was her skirt. It was all topped off with sparkling jewelry handcrafted by the Tenders-of-Himalaya, her hair done up in a cascade of white-blond. Her makeup was perfect.

She swayed up to Elana and looked her over skeptically. "Not when today is my *actual* birthday. And of course when I fence *I* wear fencing gear, and when I hunt I wear hunting gear, but I would never *think* of wearing either in the common rooms."

She turned to her friends and clapped her hands. "Come! I believe the crowd downstairs has reached critical mass, and my sister is here . . ." Katharine frowned at Elana and reached for her. "After a fashion. It will hardly be the grand entrance I wanted, but it'll have to do—" She froze.

The look of horror on her face, as she drew back her bloody hand, almost made Elana smile. "You're hurt!"

The real distress in her voice erased Elana's resentment. She looked down and saw that blood had soaked through the cotton wad and left a broad stain under her rib.

"No no, it's just my wrist, see?" She held up her arm. "Just a nick from the saber. It happens when you spar."

"Oh, no, no, let me see!" Katharine had forgotten the splendor of her costume, as well as her dance partner and the other dancers. Like the Devries sisters, they were children of the Hundred, the Million's most powerful families. She gathered one of her scarves and dabbed at Elana's arm. "Oh, it's terrible! In the old days, that would have left a scar and made you practically unmarriageable! It must hurt terribly, you poor thing."

"It only hurts when you prod it." Elana pulled herself free. "Please, they're expecting us."

"Not like that, they aren't!" Katharine pirouetted gracefully and called out, "Small emergency. Let's reconvene in the lounge in, say, five minutes?"

Katharine clapped her hands and dozens of bots came running. Two held silk-paneled privacy screens, which they slapped down on either side of Elana while another tottered in balancing fifty or so boxes of shoes, and other things arrived that she couldn't quite make out because the medbot was spraying her wrist with liquid bandage.

Elana threw out her arms and waited as the bots cut the hunter's buckskins off her body. The sweeping slices they made with their blades were so precise she didn't even feel them, and the clothing fell away without a whisper. She admired that precision; it was what she'd been striving for just now when she got this stab in the forearm. These quick, delicate movements were her focus, not her hovering sister, or the extravagance of light flooding across the furred furniture and marble sculptures, or the delicate mothbot mobile that danced in midair in the shaft of sunlight, the little wings of its many bodies tilting rainbow colors in clever patterns across the walls and ceiling.

"Today is the real birthday party, so you'll have to be perfect," Katharine said. New bots paraded into the room, each one wearing some version of this month's highest fashions. These were Alagast gowns, each sewn by Devries bots in perfect imitation of Seyna's stitch-work. The first was emerald green with a gold-chased bodice and real topazes strewn throughout the skirt. Elana barely glanced at it. The second was ruby—gems were apparently in right now—but "that's never been your color," said Katharine, and that was that. The third, a stunning white, was sewn from spider-silk lace so delicate, and done in so many layers, that its outlines shimmered on the edge of visibility. Elana finally began to take notice, but it was the last one that made her forget fencing and the annoyance of yet one more birthday party.

She felt a tug at her arm and looked down to see that while she watched the parade of gowns, the medbot had discreetly sealed and hidden the saber cut. She grunted in appreciation and turned back to look at the ensemble she was thinking of choosing.

It was black, its fabric a fullerene far more supple and lighter than the best silk. No doubt it had been woven in the past few minutes by a whole roomful of bots, just like the other outfits. As the fake wearing it moved, the material subtly stretched and tightened, resulting in a perfect moving pose. "There are muscles in the fabric?" she asked the model.

"Artificial muscles, such as ours, ma'am," it said, then curtsied.

"Twirl," commanded Elana, and the bot spun. The dress worked with that spin, compensating and perfecting the motion in all its parts. The effect was almost hallucinatory, as if dress and wearer were one organic whole.

"Oh, it's perfect!" said Katharine. She knew best about these things, so Elana nodded to the bot. She threw out her arms again, and the bots began sewing onto her body an exact match to the dress in front of her. It took only a minute or so, and then she turned on the new heels that had been slipped onto her feet.

Elana took a deep breath and went to make her entrance—on her sister's terms, not her own as she'd hoped.

Katharine was now wearing great swan's wings and twirled in the air above the ballroom. Elana chose to walk by herself down the grand sweeping stairway. The ballroom had been assembled this morning at the bottom of the vast glittering interior of the family aerostat—a two-kilometers-wide transparent sphere currently sailing a thousand meters above the Swiss Alps. Its curving sides were reinforced by beams and spars in Art Deco patterns that swept up to entwine overhead at cloud height. Built into the flanks and underside of the sphere were apartments and armories, compact factories and hangars, even a fairy castle Elana had used as her personal palace when she was younger. There were minarets and galleries, sculpture gardens and balconied groves, and swimming pools half filling smaller spheres that hung from the upper curves of the place like chandeliers. These could be reached only by crossing gently swaying rope bridges.

Swarm sculptures flocking overhead took on various fanciful forms as Elana descended. They cast shadows ahead of her in intricate moiré patterns, while her dress did its own ballet in time to her steps. Below, the ballroom was decorated with men and women in spectacular uniforms and gowns, some haloed by the glitter of their own private holographic projectors. All these people were preternaturally beautiful, and the oldest here might appear younger than their grandchildren. Cassa Fie-of-Yanassouko was dominating the dance floor in a pas de deux with Tien Wong-of-Yichang. A practiced eye could read the social gossip of the Million from who stood where, whose fan was tilted just so, and who stood to one side or laughed easily by the tables.

Elana was thinking about her footwork, and what she'd done to get herself cut.

"Elana Devries-of-Balashikha," announced a footman bot at the base of the marble steps. Some of the nearer men bowed and some women curtsied, and Elana returned the motion. How deep the bows and curtsies were—and who made them—told her all she needed to know about her family's status today.

Since these steps and bows were so much like the movements in fencing, it was easy for her to shift her attention to assessing the right opening lines to use for each person she approached. Adiema Persephus-of-Rangiroa was a technocrat, so as he took her hand she said, "I hear on some worlds they have bots to tell you where you stand socially. All this exercise would be quite unnecessary on such a planet, don't you think?"

He laughed. "Had an eyeful of it coming down the stairs, did you?" He was five times her age, and she remembered him looking exactly like this when she was an infant on his knee. "But for shame, Elana, on Earth bots like that are . . ."

She tried to remember that old, disused word. "Illegal?"

He scoffed. "Oh, worse than that! They're *gauche.*"

She smiled and detached herself, moving on to the next greeting. The next few minutes of banter were deadly serious, as was the order she took in moving around the room. Luckily it was all drearily familiar.

Elena was about to ask for a drink when she saw a bot

gesture for her attention. *Uh-oh.* It stood next to the one person in the crowd who made her more nervous than the visiting auditor: Aunt Tatiana. Reluctantly, Elana went to join her near the upward-curving outer wall of the aerostat. The sky was a faded blue dotted randomly with clouds; far below, the opal-green waters of a mountain lake beckoned.

Tatiana's pale blue eyes narrowed as she took in the dress. "Can I assume you had a run-in with your sister?"

Elana sighed and slipped off the high heels, wriggling her toes on the marble. "I had a plan and everything." She showed off her wrist, where the cut was now barely visible. "I was fencing. It was a good look. Katharine wouldn't stand for it."

"Of course not. Your sister behaved correctly. As always."

"Of course she did." Elana looked Tatiana in the eye. "That kind of behavior makes her a better pawn."

"You disapprove?"

Elana inclined her head, neither agreeing nor disagreeing. "We all accept that we play roles," she said. "It's our duty as members of the family. Katharine knows it, even if none of us have ever sat her down and told her frankly what her role is."

"Exactly. But you and I have talked many times, haven't we, niece?" Her aunt laughed lightly.

Tatiana was only a few years older than Katharine, but they were utterly different. Tatiana wasn't the heir of central Russia's Balashikha province, but nobody in the family opposed her decisions, not even Uncle Maxwell, the patriarch. She was too often right.

"And yet," Tatiana went on pensively, "I'm still not sure." She looked out briefly at the empty landscapes passing below. "You're certain you want to go through with this?"

Elana nodded. "I want to join the Human Sustainability Task Force."

"Why?"

Elana was puzzled. They'd discussed this. "Because the auditors need reform. And that can't be done from outside."

Tatiana frowned. "But why are *you* so keen on being an auditor?"

Now Elana hesitated. "I-I just think it's the right thing to do. Visitors aren't monsters. We Million breed enough of those on our own, but somehow people have taken to looking the other way and blaming outsiders for all our problems."

For a while Tatiana stared out the vast transparent wall. Then she said, "Elana, have you ever considered what it is about your own role that none of us have talked to you about?"

It took a few seconds for these words to register. Then Elana shook her head. "What? Wait, I—" She'd come to think of herself as a member of Tatiana's inner circle, albeit a junior one. She got to hear her aunt's secrets and plans. She assumed she was being groomed as one of the family's next strategists.

Tatiana laughed at her confusion. "Oh, it's fine, don't worry. There's nothing of your sister in you. You're no pawn, Elana, that's the point. What you do have is unshakable ideals, and yes, we encouraged those in you. But only because that's where your natural inclinations lay. That's what will make the combination of you and your sister unstoppable: Katharine's innocence is real, and so is your sense of justice."

Elana felt herself blushing. "Well," she said, twisting her hands together, "I guess I . . ."

"But there's still another question you haven't asked me," Tatiana went on.

"What question?"

Tatiana leaned forward. "Why, exactly, is it that I would approve of you joining the auditors?"

"Oh." Well, she had certainly worried that Tatiana *wouldn't* approve . . . "I guess I thought you agreed with me. That they need oversight."

"Hmmph. Well, stop that. You have to think *every*thing through. Why would I want my brightest niece running away to join the population police? They're about as disreputable a pack of thugs and reprobates as you could find among the Million. Nobody likes them; nobody even likes to talk about them. Keeping our population at one million is an unpleasant necessity, like treating sewage. We have to do it to satisfy our treaties with Earth's *other* civilization.

"But a Devries-of-Balashikha joining the auditors? It's a scandal! Our family is one of the Hundred! We are the richest, most powerful, most privileged people who have ever lived, and you want to join the auditors?" She threw up her hands. "Oh, it's perfect!"

Elana was thoroughly embarrassed now. "I know Father disapproves, but—"

"I talked him around. Because"—and here Tatiana's smile was impish—"we do need a family member in the auditors.

"I don't remember the last Jubilee any more than you do," she went on. "Every thirty years, for one month, Earth erupts in chaos. Ten billion people overrun the careful gardening we've been doing for the past generation. The best we Million can do is run and hide—or so most of us think. It's during that time that new conspiracies are hatched, traitors are born, dark Easter eggs are hidden in the cities and countryside—and visitors go to ground everywhere, hibernating on secret schedules to awake when we least expect.

"But Jubilee is the time of grand politics, Elana. It's when the auditors give their reports to both Earth's peoples. It's when new alliances are made and plots come to a head. In the past, the Devries have grown more powerful by steering clear of the mess. This time . . . there's no avoiding it.

"The family needs power brokers actively at the table. That's me, and your father, and the rest of us. Katharine has her role, of course. But we also need reliable intelligence. We need a spy in the machinery."

Elana gaped at her for a second, then laughed. "You're kidding."

Her aunt laughed, too. "Make no mistake, Elana, whatever your brothers and cousins do, and however popular and famous Katharine becomes through her beauty and talents, when Jubilee rolls around, you will be the kingmaker."

She looked over her shoulder, and down. "We'll be landing in a few hours. Katharine may think this grand ball is for her, but this is a great day for you, too. Make the most of it.

"And through it all, though, remember that you have a task now.

"Hand us the auditors on a silver platter," she said as the plains of northern Italy appeared ahead, "and the Balashikhas will continue to rule the world for, well . . .

"Hopefully, for the foreseeable future."

• • •

Everywhere he looked, Gavin saw proof that he should not exist.

He was traveling in a zeppelin hand-built by the Shens-of-Dalou. It could accommodate hundreds, but Gavin was the only passenger. After days of travel, much of it over empty ocean, hopeful meadows and forests were now rolling hypnotically below. Despite his misery, Gavin found himself sitting before the vast curving window at the ship's prow, watching the world unreel beneath him. He let the images stand in for thoughts; he had no more energy for those.

The Makhavs' aircar had taken him to Rochester, and not a minute passed as it flew that he didn't think about turning around and pursuing the auditors who had taken Bernie. What was he going to do if he caught up with Karelia, though? He'd been trapped his whole life by his status as a nonperson—he couldn't travel, couldn't even reveal his existence to anyone outside the family. Now he was trapped again. The sensation should be familiar, but all he could feel right now was fury.

No human presence had awaited him at the Rochester

airfield, only bots that pointed out the airship he should board. He'd had some vague thought of bolting into the underbrush at that point, but he knew he had absolutely no chance on his own. Eli Makhav-of-Winter-Park had thrown him a lifeline, however brief and uncertain it might be, and he had to take it. So even as he told himself he wouldn't do it, he'd introduced himself as Neal Makhav and walked up this airship's gangplank.

And so, thoroughly fenced in by events, thinking had become for him not just painful but useless.

Every few hundred kilometers, a bot would announce which Great Family's province they were passing over. The names were ancient: Cumbria, Leeds, Norwich. Brussels, Luxembourg, Bavaria. There were no settlements. Elephants, boars, lions, and the ancient bull of legend, the aurochs, wandered at will. Now and then the zeppelin would pass one of the museum cities—and then, despite his misery, Gavin would walk to one of the open galleries to watch it pass underneath as the headwind tore at his hair.

Often, nothing remained of the old towns but the cathedrals, which had been built to last. Some cities had been tended well, and thousands of years of architectural glory were on display, all of it lovingly tended by the bots that walked their plazas and alleys.

Dusk chased the sun into France and Iberia, and the

Alps rolled by. Their peaks were the last to catch the light, and the mountaintops blazed like a thousand bonfires for a few minutes before night fell entirely. Now the land below was invisible, cloaked in a blackness it had not seen while the cities had been inhabited. The sky blazed with stars and the Milky Way bannered across them like a conqueror's flag.

"Sir?" He looked past the row of couches that faced the curving window. The bot that announced the names of the provinces was standing in the door to the zeppelin's grand lounge. "You have an urgent call, sir, from Thomas Jagand-of-Karelia."

Gavin leaped to his feet. "Where can I take it?"

"This way."

Gavin followed the bot, cursing under his breath. In a booth with a velvet curtain, he sat and tapped the screen, and immediately, Karelia's face appeared. He looked annoyed.

"Listen, Makhav, you'll be arriving at Venice soon, and I want to make sure you and I are on the same side. Storywise, that is."

Gavin felt light-headed. His father's murderer wanted help with his alibi? It took a supreme effort for him to keep his face neutral and his voice from shaking as he said, "What do you mean?"

"Bernard Penn will be tried for the murder of his father. You will be called to testify, and . . . well, let's just say I think you have a bright future among the auditors. I hope you won't start by corroborating Bernard Penn's version of events."

Gavin made himself breathe in and out, deliberately, three times, then said, "What version of events would I be corroborating, then? Sir?"

"Well, for starters, Penn's claiming he had an illegal brother, and that you chased him off a cliff. We both know *that's not true.* Correct?"

He stared unblinkingly at Gavin. Not because he wanted to, but just because the tension became unbearable, Gavin nodded curtly.

"Good. But there's another thing. Penn's also saying that the auditors attacked the Chaffee estate without warning and that he and his brother fled."

"And . . . that's not what happened?"

"You tell me." Karelia leaned forward, his smile unpleasant. "Isn't it true that your aircar was passing the estate at the time? That you could clearly see none of the auditors' forces had landed when Bernard ran from the estate? Isn't that right?"

"Y-yes, sir." *I'll just humor him, say what he wants to hear.* "I landed because he was behaving suspiciously, and the house . . . the house was on fire . . . ?"

Karelia nodded enthusiastically. "Exactly. The auditors

didn't land until after you confronted Bernard Penn. Is that how you remember it?"

He looked Karelia straight in the eye. "Absolutely."

"Excellent. You might as well tell the story right now, and I'll record it. This will be your formal deposition for the trial. We'll speak in person when I get to Venice, but in the meantime, I'd appreciate it if you didn't talk to anyone—especially your teachers and your new classmates—about the case. Not a hint, hear?" Karelia tilted his chin down, frowning at Gavin.

Gavin nodded, mouth dry.

"Good. Let's start the deposition, then, with your name . . ."

It seemed to take forever; afterward, Gavin ran from the booth to the outside gallery. He wanted to fling himself over the rail but could only hang his head over it and retch into the rushing air.

• • •

"Sir?" Gavin started. He had been clinging to the rail for long minutes, the tumult of his emotions well matched by the turbulence of the air. Indifferent to his condition, the footman bot bowed to him. "I'm sorry to interrupt, sir, but I thought you might want to know that our destination is visible."

Gavin slumped and pushed himself away from the railing. It was too late for him to change course, so he walked to the bow and looked out. There it was, on the horizon, a tiny pool of light just four kilometers square. Once it might have been one insignificant speck in a landscape painted with lights. Now it was the only thing visible under the sky.

Venice. The only inhabited city Gavin had ever seen, and one of the three largest gatherings of human beings on Earth. There were other airships standing above that bauble of lights. Some were like the auditors' cargo ship that had brought Gavin here: three hundred meters long, gabled and galleried, and painted in intricate designs to mark the family and estate of their owners. Some were much, much bigger, like hovering cities themselves. They drifted above the canals and palaces like curious bees above a flower.

And there—he'd seen one, and there was another! There were *people* down there. His heart began to hammer as he saw just how many of them were walking these streets. Of course he'd expected it, but . . . how was he going to be able to greet all those hundreds of people? Listen to them all? Even remember their names? He turned away from the sweeping windows and waved at one of the airship's bots. "How long until we land?"

"Ten minutes, sir. Congratulations on your acceptance into the school."

"The school . . ." A school for auditors, the same people who had killed his family. He shivered and wrapped his arms around himself.

Be worthy of the Million, he told himself, imagining that it was Bernie's voice saying it. His brother's life was in his hands now—and it might rest on how well Gavin played the role of Neal Makhav in the next few minutes.

Landing was anticlimactic; suddenly the hatches sprang open and a ramp unrolled to reveal pavement below. Gavin took one step, then another, and soon found himself standing on a red carpet on the ground. Brilliant lights blinded him, and when he shielded his eyes with his hand, he made out two rows of bots lining the edges of the carpet. "Whose servants are these?" he asked the one that had served him on board the zeppelin. It had remained on the ramp.

"They are yours, sir," it said. "Your local retinue."

Now he saw that all the waiting machines wore the Winter Park colors; they were all facing him, no doubt watching for any hint that he might need something from them.

"Ah," said Gavin. He was half alarmed and half relieved. One needed a retinue, after all, to go anywhere or do anything respectable. These were hardly his own bots, though . . .

He cleared his throat. "Well, then, take me to . . . where

ever it is . . . I'm supposed to go."

The bots nodded as one, a motion so sharp he could practically hear it. Then they were moving, crisscrossing the carpet on a hundred different errands. Gavin took a tentative step down the carpet, and four of them fell smoothly into step with him.

"Hey, you!"

A young man not much older than Gavin was approaching. He had a shaved head, wore dark clothing in a severe cut, and at his side was a sheathed sword. As he loomed out of the darkness, Gavin made out dozens of white scars—everywhere, it seemed—on the backs of his hands, his exposed wrists, his neck, even his face. They looked like nicks, long-healed cuts.

So here it came. Did he look acceptable? Was his jacket straight? His hair? What was he supposed to say? Martin had drilled him in etiquette many times, he'd practiced with Bernie and the bots, but now all that experience seemed to flee. He realized he was staring slack-jawed at the youth. He forced himself to step forward. Smile. Prepare to bow.

"Good evening," said Gavin, just as he'd learned. "My name is—"

"You can't park that thing there!"

"N-Neal Makhav-of . . . ?" He looked where the black-clothed youth was pointing.

"Your airship! Move it!"

"I'm sorry. I didn't direct the airship here, nor do I own it." Gavin chose his words precisely. This kid's tone was insolent; Dad wouldn't have let Bernie use such a tone.

"You came in on it, it's yours, in't? Move it."

Now Gavin stood to his full height and crossed his arms. "Why, may I ask?"

"I don't have to explain myself to a yokel like you," sneered the other. Behind him, a retinue of similarly clothed bots were gathering in a decidedly threatening way.

Gavin cocked an eyebrow, sizing him up. "Really?"

"Really." But there it was: Gavin could see just a moment's hesitation in his eye. Then it was replaced with genuine anger. "I said move— Ow!"

A small rock twirled away, having hit him on the head. He whirled. "Who threw that?"

Gavin turned to look, too, and what he saw were two very odd things.

In the middle distance, silk-robed bots on stilts were aiming spotlights at other bots that were carrying banners, sumptuous golden chests, rolled-up carpets, and covered palanquins overspilling with pillows and couches. Some of the colorful fakes balanced golden pitchers and trays; others juggled or mimed elaborate dances. Towering a good six meters above them was a slowly moving majestic robot elephant, festooned with jewels, draped with golden tapestries, with a turret sprouting from its back. A telescope wobbled in its mount there, but there was nobody sitting on the purple velvet seats under its bulbous roof.

Much nearer, silhouetted by this vision, an unruly mob of people was bobbing and weaving in silent threat.

A mob of short, skinny people, it seemed.

From somewhere in the crowd, a reedy voice shouted, "Pick on somebody of your own ugliness, Bland!"

"Oh, it's *you."* The bald-headed guy (Bland?) put one hand on the pommel of his sword and spat. "Ross Donegal. Still too much of a coward to come out of your cloud of fakes."

So that was what Gavin was seeing. The mob was all bots, identical copies of some thin-faced, sail-eared boy with a crop of sandy hair and a fierce expression. It was impossible to tell which was the real one, and they were all popping off expressions and poses—emotes—like little emotional lightning bolts.

"He said it wasn't his airship," called the voice again.

Another voice interrupted. "Besides, Jerome, why do you care where he parks?"

This speaker was a tall, slender youth; his mop of hair was black and he had coffee-colored skin. He wore the same bright silks as the bots that were crowding around the mechanical elephant.

"Hemandar, I might have known that was your contraption clotting up the runway," said Jerome Bland. "I suppose you hand-built it, like you do all your bots? Well, color me unimpressed. It's in the way!"

Hemandar bowed to Gavin; suddenly and simultaneously, all the Ross Donegals did, too. "I apologize for our classmate," said Hemandar. Turning to Bland, he said, "And yet, you still haven't explained why I should care where we go."

"Because!" Bland pointed at the sky, as though Gavin, Ross, and Hemandar were imbeciles. *"She's coming!"*

Hemandar gaped up at something behind Gavin. Confused, he turned, to find that somehow the sun hadn't finished setting—or sunrise had come ten hours early. His zeppelin was silhouetted by a vast tower of peach- and rose-colored cloud whose outskirts were lit by flickering lightning. Or was it lightning?

"Oh! . . . What's she playing?" Hemandar nudged one of the Rosses, who snapped his fingers. Another Ross stepped out and the first said, "Find her live feed."

The fake nodded, and suddenly music flooded the dark lot. It was magnificent, with a thrumming drumbeat underlying a full-throated orchestra and choir, and atop it all the soaring, diving voice of a solo woman performer.

The song was electrifying—Gavin had never heard anything like it—and the lightning snapped the sides of the glowing thunderhead in perfect time.

Bland planted his feet wide and crossed his arms, frowning at the sky. Ross and Hemandar whooped in delight, and despite himself Gavin found he was grinning. The thunderhead was *dancing*!

Bland sent Gavin a scowl. "You need to scamper out of the way now. One of the Hundred is coming!"

The gorgeous thunderhead slid grandly across the sky until it stood next to the crescent moon. Then, at a climax in the music, dozens of brilliant darts shot out of it, each one trailing a thin thread of light. They wove together, making a complex knot in the sky, then ducked and dove at the landing field.

They were golden jet aircraft. Gavin just had time to admire their sleek, menacing shapes before they flashed past, and he was knocked off his feet by a clap of sound like nothing he'd ever felt in his life.

Bland was on his feet, but Ross and Hemandar had fallen over, too. They were laughing as they rose. Gavin stood, letting bots brush him off as the jets swung around for another pass, the music peaked, and something emerged from the embrace of the cloud.

It was an airship, but it was nothing like the Shen-of-Dalou piece he'd ridden in. This was a floating city with towers that trailed like the tendrils of a jellyfish beneath a vast translucent sphere that must be two kilometers across. The sphere was lit from inside—the light banging in time to the music—and below were garlanded strings of color. Acrobots twirled and dove between trapezes, and a thousand more clouded around it, some shaped like fabulous glowing birds, others simply confections of radiant light. Open stairways and bridges connected its towers and balconies; here and there he could see human-shaped forms standing on golden balconies. One waved and, without thinking, he waved back.

The aerostat descended, the music reached its climax, and suddenly, all was dark. He could actually hear the last echoes of music bouncing off buildings and the sides of zeppelins as the aerial city—now dark—lowered its last few meters to the ground.

But above it . . . The hairs on the back of Gavin's neck stood up as he saw what had happened in the sky.

"The moon, the moon!" a Ross was howling. He'd grabbed Hemandar's shoulder and was pointing. "Look at it! Just look!"

In the darkness within the moon's crescent, a glowing smiley face had appeared.

They must be projecting that image onto the shadowed side of Luna using one of the Million's orbital laser systems. But the sheer power, both political and electrical, required to light thousands of kilometers of lunar mountain, crater, and rill, just to make an entrance . . .

The smiley face winked. Then it went out.

With a start, Gavin realized he was standing shoulder to shoulder with Hemandar and one of the Rosses, in almost total darkness, with nothing in his ears but the creak of distant ropes and cricket-song.

"Wh—" His voice squeaked, and he coughed and tried again. "Who is that?"

Jerome Bland barked a contemptuous laugh. "The one whose rightfully grand entrance you almost spoiled." He sniffed. He began striding across the landing field in the direction of the giant mass that blotted out half the sky.

Hemandar clapped a hand on Gavin's shoulder and grinned. "Don't mind Jerome, he's always like that." He began walking, too, with Rosses trailing him, and his brightly lit elephant lurched into motion. Looking back, he saw that Gavin hadn't moved, and said, "Come along, oh great Neal Makhav-of. And you can meet her, too."

"Meet who?"

"*Her,* of course! Katharine Devries-of-Balashikha."

• • •

Lights on the aerostat began coming on again—first the colored strings, then pale footlights on the bridges and outside stairways, and finally the amber glow of interior lamps. Gavin could see bots hurrying back and forth, and numerous human shapes moving more languidly.

Ground cars pulled into place under the airship. Some carried bots, but young men and women piled out of one. They laughed and waved as they grabbed mooring lines from the bots and winched down the ship's grand staircase. Up there at its top, four people had appeared.

A crowd of Rosses pushed Gavin forward, and they arrived at the head of the line just as the staircase made contact with the ground and the figures above began strolling down it. Floodlights blinked on, and as the bots unrolled a crimson carpet and scattered rose petals on it, the heirs of the Balashikha territory stepped onto Venetian soil.

Two were older adults, the man dressed in a fine suit and the woman in a glittering ball gown. They scanned the crowd of approaching young people, and indifferently turned away.

The other two, though . . .

Ross's hand clipped Gavin on the back of the head. "Close yer mouth, you fool," he muttered.

Katharine Devries-of-Balashikha was wearing an off-the-shoulder confection made of fine black satin, with a dusting of pearls winding around it. Her hair was piled up and held in place with silver pins. She was the most beautiful woman Gavin had ever seen.

Jerome Bland strode up, swept his scabbard back, and bowed gracefully, then extended a hand. "Katharine!" She ignored the hand and embraced him, and over his shoulder, she smiled at Hemandar, Gavin, and the Rosses.

"Jerome, it's good to see you," she said, breaking free. "And this must be Ross Donegal-of-Cavan! And Hemandar Satna-of-Amravati, how are you?" She turned back to Bland. "Is it true? Did you really decide to join the auditors because of my sister?"

Bland growled. "I believe you'll find she joined because of me."

"He would say that," murmured a voice at Gavin's side. He started and looked down at the young woman who'd suddenly appeared at his side.

"But Ross, Hemandar, where are your manners?" said Katharine. She swept up to Gavin, and when she smiled, two endearing dimples appeared on either side of her mouth.

Jerome Bland cleared his throat. "Oh, that, yes, this is, uh—"

If ever in his life he needed to remember the lessons in etiquette he'd so hated as a kid, now was the time. Gavin took the half step forward that he'd been made to practice again and again, tilted his head just so, and then he executed two deep bows—the first to Katharine Devries, the second to the other young lady. "Neal Makhav-of-Winter-Park, at your service," he said, and it would all have been perfect had his voice not trailed off into something of a squeak at the end. But when he straightened up, he saw that Jerome Bland was scowling at him, and he took that as a good sign. Katharine Devries curtsied and smiled at him from under her long black lashes.

"And what brings you to Venice, Neal Makhav?"

"Ah, as to that—" He didn't know what to say and ended up waving one hand helplessly at Hemandar and the Rosses. Katharine's eyes widened.

"You're becoming an auditor, too?" He managed a nod. As Bland glared at him, Katharine swayed and reached past him to draw out the other girl.

"I feel so much better to see that you'll all be here," said Katharine. "Jerome has met my sister, Elana, but I'm afraid none of you have. She'll be studying with you!"

Where Katharine's gown was black as the sky, Elana's was silver. Where Katharine's was revealing, hers covered her arms and swept up to hide her throat. Elana Balashikha was shorter than her sister, but while Katharine dominated the crowd with her beauty, Elana possessed a different kind of magnetism. Though she was pretty, her face was built for serious expressions, with a small mouth and dark eyes presided over by severely drawn eyebrows.

She didn't stand; she poised, as if about to launch herself into some fierce action. When Katharine introduced her, she didn't step forward but gave a half bow, smiled, and said nothing.

"Well," said Hemandar, "that's . . ."

"Have you come a long way?" Gavin asked impulsively. The three boys glared at him, but Elana smiled, a sudden radiance.

"Our estate's in central Asia," she said. "It took us a few days to get here."

"These three were cluttering up the landing field," said Bland. "I tried to get them out of the way for you, but—"

Katharine laughed and threw up her hands. "Oh! The sacrifices I make for a decent entrance." She leaned in to Bland. "Did you know that . . . vessel"—she arched an eyebrow at the city-sized airship—"doesn't even have a playhouse with proper acoustics? I haven't rehearsed in days."

As Bland shook his head in sympathy, Elana Devries caught Gavin's eye, and he wasn't sure of it, but wasn't that a long-suffering smile that flickered, for just a second, across her face?

"Well, let's not dawdle on this drafty slab when the city beckons!" Katharine turned and strode decisively toward the distant glittering skyline. Bots leaped into action, wrestling huge packages onto their shoulders and following as best they could.

"Would you like to ride my elephant?" Hemandar asked Katharine.

She waved a negligent hand. "Have one," she said. "I'm sure something novel will appear."

She marched toward the canal that separated the airship docks from the city proper. She would have walked straight into the water had a frenzied mob of bots not built a pontoon bridge for her. She ignored them and simply strolled, confident that they would neither let her come to harm nor fail to give her the direct route she wanted to the city. The whole crowd of Rosses was watching her go with expressions of astonishment on its faces. Jerome Bland strode up to Elana, stopped and clicked his heels, and cocked his arm in apparent expectation that she would take it.

She turned to Hemandar Satna. "Well, *I* would like an elephant ride. If you're still offering."

"Ah. Of course." Hemandar bowed to her, not looking up at Bland, who stood stiffly at attention. "Coming, Makhav?" Hemandar said to Gavin.

"Thanks, but I think I'll find my own way."

"Suit yourself. Classes start tomorrow. Nine sharp!"

Gavin smiled and nodded. He was thinking that if he did show up to the auditor headquarters in the morning, he should do so armed and demanding justice. He would see them answer for what they'd done.

As he turned to go, he glimpsed Elana Devries-of-Balashikha looking like she wanted to say something to him, but she didn't, and he kept going, into his own crowd of waiting servants. They had an amphibious car ready for him. He climbed into it gratefully, wanting nothing more than to escape from all these new people, and from any thought about what might happen tomorrow.

• • •

He'd known in a vague sort of way that Venice was special; so were all the ancient places preserved by the Million. He'd never imagined a place so exotic and beautiful as this. The city was like one single, gigantic work of art, with a wonder around every corner; even having canals instead of streets seemed apt, and deliberately provocative. Gavin could see why the Million would choose to reside here. The place challenged everyone who entered it to do better, be better than they were. For the Million, determined as they were to match or exceed everything humanity had ever accomplished, Venice was a worthy symbol.

His bots kept him moving in an efficient convoy down the quiet, dappled waterways. Pastel light and tinted shadows leaned across the water, and gauze curtains in the many open windows teased him with random motions. Music and murmured conversations drifted on the warm night air. His throng of boats encountered many other watercraft, and when Gavin saw other humans in them, he straightened. Some of the boats were long and narrow, with tall figureheads at each end. His bots called these "gondolas," which had a familiar ring to it. Still, he had no idea who had built this mad floating city, or when. He was too tired to ask his retinue, though surely they would have been happy to tell him.

"This will be your residence," one announced as they pulled up next to a crumbling stone dock. Gavin gawked up at the bright orange façade of a four-story building that was crammed in between two taller structures. His place tried to make up for its lack of height by sporting some sort of wildly complicated sculpture atop it—something with giant seashells and half-naked women, and a massively muscled man rearing up out of it all.

He waved away the helping hand offered by the bot and clambered out of the bobbing boat as he craned his neck to get a better look at the place. All the windows were dark. "Is this all I've got?"

"Eli Makhav-of-Winter-Park considered that it would be an appropriate size for you."

"It's tiny. Does it even have its own factories?"

Bots carrying furniture and boxes were pouring past him like he was a rock in a stream. The one next to him cocked its head in a very humanlike way and said, "Factory space can be built outside of town if you wish, sir. These are treaty-protected buildings and cannot be permanently altered. We can, however, provide any signs of life you might require. Music, sounds of conversation from the Winter Park estate. We could even leave plates of half-eaten food around if that would—"

"Forget it." He crossed his arms, wishing Bernie were here with him. Of course, Bernie had probably been to Venice before; *he* had grown up able to travel, after all.

While he stood there, the bots threw open the doors and now they were turning on lights as they moved in. Gavin reluctantly followed them and saw that the place was half furnished already. The style was ancient and ornate. He entered and found himself in a giant hall, two stories high, with a gallery wrapping around it near the painted ceiling. Bots were lighting a fire in the walk-in fireplace, but what dominated the room was a large marble statue of Zeus or somebody. Gavin made the mistake of glancing up at the ceiling, and proceeded to stand there with his mouth open for a long minute, staring at the glorious sky painted across it.

"You'll give yourself away doing that."

He jerked in surprise and looked around. The voice had been human, not a bot's, but there was no one else in the room. "What . . . ?"

"Are you gonna stare at everybody's ceiling? 'Cause this one's not that great."

The big marble statue crossed its arms and frowned down at him in apparent disapproval. Spreading its broad arms, it hopped off its meter-high pedestal. The whole palace shook with the force of its landing.

Now Gavin recognized the features carved on the stone face. "Eli Makhav. Sir."

Eli's scowl could have withered a rose garden. "What, did you expect me to use one of those primitive screens to call you?" He was visiting by telepresence—common enough among people who despised virtual, remote, and digital communications. The statue was a robot under his control.

He looked Gavin up and down. "No comment? Right, then. What's your name, boy?"

Gavin eyed the door. He could never make it in time, and if the statue had wanted him dead, he already would be. "Gavin Penn-of-Chaffee. Sir." He realized he was standing at attention and, resentful, forced himself to change his pose. He hooked a thumb in his belt and lifted his chin against Makhav's disapproving gaze.

"Thought so," said Makhav, and Gavin forgot his resentment.

"W-what do you mean? How did you—"

"Did you kill my nephew? Or was it your brother?"

"No—I mean, neither of us!" Gavin opened his mouth to explain, but how could he? Thinking back, it all seemed dreamlike now.

Eli Makhav's eyes narrowed, and Gavin realized that he must be taking his silence for guilt. "It was an accident," he blurted. "He was going to shoot me. Bernie jumped him to stop him. They fell—"

Makhav cursed and made a cutting motion with his hand. He looked away, frowning. Then he said, "That auditor, Karelia, said it was just you and Bernie on that hillside. Bernie now stands accused of murdering his own father; well, that would be your father, too, wouldn't it? He stands to lose his inheritance and his lands if it's proved, and you . . . you don't even officially exist."

"You can't let them convict Bernie of this! It was Karelia! We have to come forward, I'll tell them who I am—"

Eli was shaking his head. "Won't work," he said. "They'll never believe you."

"But you . . . you know about me? You could vouch for me!"

"Even if I did, I have no proof that you or Bernie *didn't*

kill Martin. No, you were hiding before, and you're going to keep hiding."

Gavin glared at him. "Why? Did you send the auditors after us? Or was it Neal? And why didn't you turn me in right then and there? Why let them think I was Neal Makhav? Are you after the Chaffee lands?"

A broad smile split Eli Makhav's weathered face. "You've just been bursting to ask that, haven't you?" As quick as it had appeared, the smile vanished. "You don't need to know why I'm not turning you in. All you need to know is that I'm holding it over your head. You do exactly what I say, and I'll let you continue to be Neal Makhav. A few years of that, maybe it'll even stick."

"Y-years? But *why?*"

"Because I need you to do some dirty work for me. Not the sort of thing I'd send a bot to do, and not the sort of thing any self-respecting citizen of the Million would agree to.

"You, on the other hand . . . I can discard you anytime I want. I've told the bots around you that you are Neal, but I've covered my tracks. If I decide to deny this conversation, it will look like *you* hacked the Makhav bots. There'll be no record of this call. If anybody asks about the other day, I'll say I was confused when I told the auditors I recognized you. It was . . . the dust you were covered in." Again the smile came and went.

"Meanwhile, you need to steer clear of Neal Makhav's cousins. Not that any of them are in the City, thank God. My brother doesn't leave Winter Park. The Makhavs generally hate large gatherings; I'm the only one who's used that house you're in. And, after the fight Neal had with my brother before he left, no one's going to find it odd if those two never speak again." Makhav shrugged. "This could work—if you hold up your end of the bargain . . . and that includes doing what Neal swore to his father he would do."

It took a moment for Gavin to realize what Makhav meant. "No!" He walked up to stare the statue in the eye. "You want me to *actually become* an auditor? After they killed my father? When my brother's life is at stake? I'd rather they caught me, too. My father—"

"Would want you to find out why they attacked. He'd want you to track down his killer, don't you think? He'd want you to free Bernie, wouldn't he?"

Gavin blinked at Makhav, who gave an impatient sigh and jabbed a huge finger into Gavin's chest. "You and I and Bernard know that the auditors killed your father. Nobody else does. Neal Makhav desperately wants to become an auditor, so you won't cross them. Bernie's the only loose end they know of, and they think they have that tied up. That gives us a window of opportunity to investigate the murder ourselves."

Gavin stared at him, thinking quickly. "You'd really help me do that?"

"Son, your father was a friend of mine. What do you expect?"

Gavin examined Makhav's serious face. He clenched his fists.

Eli went on. "Neal's father and I are going to engage the best treaty lawyer among the Hundred. Maybe we can make a case that it really was an illegal son who killed Martin. If the prosecution produces some fake recording of Martin claiming it's Bernie, we'll say he was confused. Whatever, we'll give them a damned good fight, believe me.

"I'll send you your first assignment tomorrow, and if you pass, I'll want you to investigate some other things for me. I need an agent in the City, one who's willing to take the kinds of risks no self-respecting, pampered child of the Million would ever take. It'll be dangerous, and you could be caught—or killed. I won't lie to you, this will be hard. But you have an opportunity here to investigate Martin's death, and there's no better base of operations for you than the auditors' school."

Gavin scowled and turned, paced a bit. For all he knew, Eli Makhav was responsible for calling the auditors in to destroy the Chaffee estate. Maybe that was how Neal had known to go there—Eli had sent him. Whatever the case, Gavin would be in no position to learn the truth if he turned down Makhav's offer.

He would find some way of turning the situation around. "I'll consider it," he said after a long pause.

Makhav barked a laugh. "Well, consider this. Bernie's in Venice." Makhav laughed again. "The auditors' school is located where the auditors are located. Venice is their home base, didn't you realize that?

"Don't get any bright ideas about breaking him out. The only way you're going to be able to see him is if you show up for class tomorrow, bright and early. Try anything, and I'm cutting you loose." He walked back to his pedestal, then paused. "I suppose you're expecting to sleep on it?" Gavin shook his head, puzzled. "Well, don't," Makhav went on. "While you were dawdling along on that airship, I was shipping out every photo, recording, and piece of memorabilia about Neal that I have. Plus a copy of the Winter Park constitution and treaties. When you show up for school tomorrow, I want you to know him inside and out—and know exactly where this family stands among the Million. You have to *be* Neal Makhav. Understand?"

"What about Bernie's trial? I'm supposed to testify. Isn't Neal's father going to be there for that?"

"No." The look on Makhav's face was ugly. "I'll make sure of that, you have my word. Too much is at stake. He won't expose you, and you won't back out now."

Defiance crumbling in the face of sheer exhaustion, Gavin nodded.

"Good luck," said Makhav, though it sounded like an insult. The statue climbed onto its pedestal, posed regally, and froze in place.

• • •

"At least I'm not the only one who partied all night," said Ross Donegal as Gavin walked up. "You look awful. And where's your ride?" There was only one Ross here, doubtless the real one, and he kept shifting nervously from foot to foot, looking around. A number of vehicles were arriving at the grand square that fronted the Doge's Palace. Gavin could even see Hemandar Satna's elephant clumsily climbing out of some sort of barge. Young men and women were gathering under a tall banner near the palace.

"I walked," he replied to Donegal.

Ross took a second look, then burst out laughing. "What are you, going to a funeral?" Gavin had chosen clothing that was light and easy to move in, reasoning that an auditor's job was much like a hunter's. He couldn't imagine hunting in the pastel blue waistcoat and knee pants that Ross was wearing.

There was a loud *crack!* from the direction of the banner pole. Gavin was grateful for the distraction. A tall man dressed even more severely than he was stood there, flanked by two big, glossy black battle mechs. "Attention!" he shouted. "Fall into line. You will enter the palace single file, with no bots, no theatrics, and no talking! You're alive only because we take what we do seriously. It's your turn to do the same."

Gavin went to the head of the line, relieved that he wouldn't have to introduce himself right now to each and every one of the hundred or so students. Some were being sent off by their parents or friends; some had musical retinues that they were now shushing; others were muttering together in frank disbelief that anyone should use such a tone of voice on *them*. There were a few, though, who looked serious and interested, and they quickly fell in behind Gavin.

"Follow me," said the severe man. Then he raised an eyebrow at the crowd of still-talking dandies. "Or not," he added. "But this is your only chance to join the auditors. Come, or go." He turned on his heel and stalked toward the palace. The battle bots wheeled about and followed, and so did Gavin.

"Good morning, Neal," someone said behind him. He looked back to find Elana Balashikha behind him. He paused to let her catch up, bowing slightly.

"Good morning," he said. "I'm afraid I don't know all these people."

She looked back, puzzled. "I don't know them either."

"But shouldn't we . . . be introduced?"

A knowing look crossed Elana's face. "Not used to crowds, are you? Look, just pretend they're fakes. We'll all get to know each other in time, but even then you shouldn't expect to remember *every*body's name."

He thought about that while they passed out of the sunlight and into the Doge's Palace. There were many more people inside, all older adults. They looked very purposeful, bustling about or standing together talking in quiet tones. Gavin and Elana fell silent in their presence.

The battle bots were surprisingly nimble and quiet on the stairs, but since they stood a good two heads taller than any human, it was impossible to lose track of them. Gavin allowed his gaze to drift to the opulent architecture and décor of the palace. Everything was gold, or finely painted pastoral scenes, or intricately carved stone.

This was how he'd always pictured the Million, as the capstone of every dream of wealth and power that humanity had ever had. They owned the world. And each and every one of them had at his or her disposal more riches than the greatest emperor or billionaire from the past.

Except that this wasn't entirely true. The Million lived under a shadow. Every thirty years they were reminded of just how insignificant they could become if they were to relax their vigilance, or fail in any one of their many duties. It hung over them, never talked about, studiously ignored, that they were simply caretakers. Earth's real owners would be back, and soon, and when they arrived the place had better be in good condition.

Upstairs they trod marble halls to the back of the palace, where a side entrance led to a covered bridge of white stone. Elana hopped up and down when she saw it. She pointed excitedly and whispered to Gavin, "The Bridge of Sighs!"

He smiled politely. Seeing his lack of recognition, she fell back to walk beside him. "It's how they led prisoners from the courts to the prison. They called it the Bridge of Sighs because it's where you'd get your last look at the city."

They filed onto the bridge and he dutifully glanced out one of the carved stone windows. "Legend says that if lovers kiss in a gondola under the bridge at sunset, their love will be eternal," Elana continued. "Now this up ahead is Piombi prison. Casanova was imprisoned here, and he escaped by digging a hole in the floor!"

She spoke the names and told the stories with pride, as if these stones and their history were her own. Well,

Gavin mused, if you truly felt the Million's sense of ownership over places like this, you probably thought they were.

"Single file!" The voice from ahead snapped him back to attention, and he fell behind Elana again. She shot him an apologetic smile, and then they stepped inside the darkness of the Piombi. Gavin heard someone new come beside him.

"Single file," he hissed at the newcomer, but there was no response. After a few moments they emerged into a low corridor lit by amber lamps. Gavin turned to see that he was being accompanied by a robot. Its blank oval face swiveled as if it were looking back at him.

Elana had a similar bot walking next to her; so did all the other students. All these mechanicals were dressed in black livery, the colors of the auditors—but there was something about the way they moved, an almost human grace Gavin found faintly disturbing.

They filed into an amphitheater, typically opulent. Uniformed men and women were waiting on the stage. Elana went to sit in the front row. Gavin hesitated. The bot next to him swiveled its head again, as if noting this. He cursed under his breath and went to sit next to her. They were flanked by the bots that had followed them.

On stage, a tall, gray-haired woman clapped her hands for silence. "Please be seated," she said. "And welcome to the Human Sustainability Task Force. I am Isabel Tuyuc-of-Cuzco, the dean of this school. I run one of the most demanding programs in the Million's educational system—but then, the Task Force has one of the most demanding jobs in the world. If you make it through the program, you'll be joining the elite who make the rest of our civilization possible. We safeguard the Million and the locksteps in equal measure, and you'll learn how one cannot be protected without protecting the others."

Gavin shifted uncomfortably in his seat. Again, the bot beside him seemed to take notice.

After talking about the nobility of the cause they were enlisting in, and the tremendous responsibility they were about to take on, Tuyuc-of-Cuzco said, "It's therefore my pleasure to introduce your instructors for this term. Your theory professor will be Haixi Bang." An elderly Oriental gentleman bowed.

"There's a *theory* for hunting vizies?" It was Jerome Bland's voice, coming from right behind Gavin. He ignored the quip and kept his eyes on the dean.

"Your arms instructor will be Tony Cupun-of-Iqaluit." Cupun was handsome, with black hair and a handlebar mustache that twitched from side to side as he smiled at the students. "Hand-to-hand will be taught by Ingrid Kena Guyot." More than petite, she was tiny—little more than a meter and a half tall. As she stepped forward,

Gavin heard Bland guffaw; her eyes instantly found the source of the sound.

"Would you like an early lesson, Master Bland?" Her voice was a feline purr.

"My apologies, ma'am," said Bland. Elana grinned at Gavin.

Dean Tuyuc-of-Cuzco shot Jerome a look as well, and Gavin heard a sliding sound that was probably Bland sinking down in his seat.

"Surveillance and investigation will be by Destiny Kolwezi." She was very tall, with long features and utterly black skin. Gavin had never seen skin like it in real life, and he found her striking and beautiful. But . . . surveillance? She was going to teach them to spy on people?

"That's it, for this term." The dean smiled again, but it wasn't a friendly smile. "This is your shakedown term. Some of you won't make the cut, and we want to find out who you are as quickly as possible. We won't waste our time or yours. Your housebots have been given your schedule and supply list; your first class starts here in one hour. Any questions?"

There was a momentary silence. Then she nodded to someone in the back row. "Yes, Kaya?"

"Ma'am, what are *these* for?" Everybody turned, including Gavin. The young lady was pointing at the robot sitting next to her.

"I'm glad you asked," said the dean. "That's your shadow."

People looked at one another blankly.

"For the next six months, that bot will accompany you everywhere," said Tuyuc-of-Cuzco. "And I mean everywhere. It will watch your every move, and learn your habits and way of thinking." She raised a hand over the sudden babble of protesting voices. "Rest assured, it won't report anything to us or any other human being. That level of surveillance isn't allowed by any Million treaty. What it learns, your shadow will keep to itself. But you will need it if you want to pass the term, because it will be the one delivering the final exam."

Now there was total silence. "The exam will consist of two parts," Tuyuc-of-Cuzco went on. "In the first part, you will have to hide, and the bot—knowing you as it does—has to find you. For the second part of the exam, your shadow will hide somewhere, and you have to find it."

"That doesn't sound too hard," Ross muttered.

"Somewhere *on Earth,"* added Tuyuc-of-Cuzco. "But it could be anywhere."

There were mutters of disbelief now.

"This is to teach you how to think like visitors, whom you will be hunting if you graduate."

There was a new, uncomfortable silence. Gavin realized he'd bitten his lip. Absently, he wiped it on his sleeve, and his shadow noticed. He inched back from the eyeless regard of the bot.

He couldn't go through with this—this shadow was going to find out who he really was for sure. But as he put his hands on the armrests to push himself to his feet, he realized that walking out would be even more suspicious than staying. He was trapped. Cursing under his breath, he sank into his seat.

The shadow took note of this, too.

It was hard to concentrate, much less sit still, through the rest of the introductions and explanations of schedules, key dates, and milestones. When a break was called, all the students bolted from the room to talk loudly in the hallway about what it all might mean. Their agendas, textbooks, and research tools had been sent to their palaces and studies. A few students were taking notes in journals, but most wanted to talk—about the program, about the final exams, about their shadows, and what they might mean.

Gavin said a few polite hellos, but he felt overwhelmed by all these people, so he ended up standing by himself near a marble pillar whose lower span had been polished and grooved by centuries of passing hands.

Only one person was left on the stage as they returned to their seats. Professor Destiny Kolwezi rocked on her heels, her hands behind her back, waiting for the stragglers. As the last laggard took his place at the back of the theater, Kolwezi held up one hand for silence.

"My name is Destiny Kolwezi," she said. "I am an auditor. And a visitor."

• • •

Gavin sucked in a too-quick breath and started coughing; the rest of the audience had gasped as well, and now everybody was talking at once. Gavin looked around hastily, but nobody was looking at him down in the corner of the third row.

Kolwezi held up her slender dark hand again.

"I am a visitor," she said. "But it's not a crime to *be* a visitor. It's only a crime for visitors to come and go or trade in secret, or smuggle, or otherwise move among us without our knowledge."

There was an attentive silence now, broken only by the blat of a boat's horn on the canal outside. Pacing along the lip of the stage, she said, "What is a visitor? Who can tell me?"

"Extra people," someone shouted. "The million-and-oneth person," somebody else said. "Secret families," said a third. "Locksteppers," added a fourth. "Martians and other spacers." Kolwezi nodded.

"Anybody who's not one of the Million, in other words. There are as many different kinds of visitors as there *are* visitors. Some, as somebody just said, are children born out of treaty, who raise the Million's population above, well, the magic number. Of course, people are born and die every day; your number fluctuates and is almost never exactly a million. But it's not supposed to stay above that level. Extra births could lead to such a problem. So the secret child is one form of visitor.

"There are occasional visitors from the other planets. Earth is mostly off-limits to them, but sometimes they come down in secret to poach. They steal rare life-forms, perform stunts for points in the attention economies . . . the list is endless. They can be really damaging to the ecosystem. There is a cordon in Earth orbit, and some of you will eventually be keeping watch over that.

"But the most troublesome visitors come from somewhere else. You all know where."

Lockstep 360/1. Earth's other civilization. The new students eyed one another, but no one wanted to say the words.

"Ten billion people!"

Kolwezi shouted these words. Now she paced the stage, obviously enjoying her audience's discomfort. "There are *ten billion* people on Earth right now, in addition to the Million. They've always been here. They were here before you were born, before your grandparents were born, and before theirs. They will be here after your grandchildren are long dead. And they are the beginning and end of everything you do, whether you want to admit it or not.

"Twenty-eight years they've been sleeping in their cicada beds, in the forbidden caverns that lie under every one of Earth's cities. A million sleep not more than a kilometer from this very spot. A kilometer, mind you, straight down . . .

"In two years they will awake, all on the same morning. They will overrun Earth for one month, then go dormant again for the next thirty years. So the locksteppers stride into the future, each step a generation in our terms, three hundred and sixty of our years for every one of theirs. They do this to sustain Earth as the garden we all wish it to be, and they do it because this hibernation cycle gives them access to the stars."

Faster than light travel was impossible. Visiting another star system took decades for even the fastest starship. If you were born into a lockstep, those decades could seem to pass in a single night. Lockstep 360/1 participated in a culture that spanned dozens of stars and thousands of planets. The price they paid was to leave normal time behind.

"They race into the future, awake one month out of

every thirty years. Yet in that month, what mischief they do!"

Kolwezi called for examples, and the students were more than happy to supply them. If you were poor among the ten billion locksteppers, you could be rich in the underpopulated Earth of the Million—if you could manage to wake off-schedule. If you'd committed a crime in one world, you might escape into the other. Things that were trash to the Million might be treasures among the locksteppers, and vice versa. A lockstepper might mess with the timer of his or her cicada bed, wake up after ten years rather than thirty, and join other conspirators among the Million. Conspiracies abounded.

"There are the expansionists!" They thought the Million should be a round Billion, the better to face the locksteppers on an equal footing.

"Don't forget the minimalists!" They thought a single family, no more than a hundred people, could take care of the whole Earth. The planet was overcrowded, in their eyes.

"The transhumanists!" They wanted to bring back artificial superintelligence. "The genocides!" Kill all the locksteppers while they slept. "Sleeping beauties!" Break the clock. Just let the locksteppers sleep a few centuries, while the Million gathered strength to force a better treaty with them. "Automators!" These were locksteppers who didn't trust the Million and would prefer the world were tended by bots and empty of people while they slept.

"Tourists!" "Vandals!" "Kidnappers!" The list went on and on. Finally, Kolwezi held up her hand. "Enough. I am a lockstepper myself. Yes, I am *that* kind of visitor—and that kind of auditor. You keep tabs on us, and we keep tabs on you. That's the treaty.

"But there's more to my story," she continued. "I wasn't born into the lockstep, but here, to a secret family among the Million. The Kolwezis were a big clan, and they lived on rich land. This was . . . many centuries ago; there are no Kolwezis today. These ones, they knew their land could sustain thousands—millions—of people, and they didn't like the interfering Million telling them how many children they could have. So they had secret pregnancies, and created a secret village where they could raise us children away from the eyes of the auditors. I don't know the whole plan, but"—she shrugged—"they hoped to breed a big enough population to challenge the treaties governing central Africa. If Kolwezi could become its own country, with thousands instead of dozens of inhabitants, then maybe we could break away from the Million. Grow more, and someday we might even challenge the lockstep."

There was outraged muttering again in the seats behind Gavin. He didn't share that particular outrage. If anything, he was intrigued. "Of course it wasn't *my* plan," the professor added. "I was born into it, as were my brothers and sisters. We were the pawns and victims of the conspiracy. They taught us that we'd be the ancestors of a new civilization, that we'd be worshiped as gods by our future descendants . . . But really, we hadn't been asked to be what we were.

"And of course, one day the auditors came. Sorry, the *Human Sustainability Task Force*." She leaned on the words with heavy irony. "We were rounded up and separated. Some of the elders fought, and some were killed." She looked down. "We were taken deep underground, to a cold, dark cavern filled with racks of silent, coffinlike machines. I was forced into one. I remember screaming, certain I was entering the land of the dead. Yet when I awoke, it was to a world of billions of people, humming with life and energy.

"I had been exiled to the lockstep." When she looked up again she seemed, of all things, amused. "So tell me, whom should I hate for that?"

Nobody else seemed to have the courage to reply, so Gavin stuck up his hand.

"Us," he said, barely keeping his voice from betraying the fury he felt. "You should hate *us*. The Million."

He looked around and saw that the other students

were trying to stare at both him and Kolwezi at once.

Kolwezi blinked at him, then her white teeth showed in a huge smile. "But you're absolutely right . . . Neal, is it?" He nodded sullenly, surprised by her reaction. The others were muttering again.

"You might be right," said Kolwezi. "*But*, let me tell you something. It's about a particularly nasty trick that bad people play on good people." Now she was scowling, pacing the stage like some tall, graceful bird. "If you want to get away with doing something—something terrible—arrange it so that stopping you requires that innocent people suffer. That way, you make the righteous people who caught you into the bad guys. Like, say you want to get away with bringing visitors into the world. Just ensure that those children are blameless—well, they will be anyway, won't they! Once they exist, they're an accomplished fact, you can't punish *them* without becoming the villain. And this, the conspirators rely on."

Gavin shook his head. "But there's no solution to that—"

"Oh, yes there is, Neal Makhav. The solution is to be the villain, because otherwise the conspirators will use the same trick again and again until they win everything. Without the Human Sustainability Task Force—without you, or who you will become—there is nothing to prevent such tragedies becoming common . . . and if they did, our treaties—between my lockstep and your Million—could unravel."

Gavin sat back, struggling to turn his glare into an indifferent mask. Stupid to have spoken up!

Kolwezi looked away again, for a long moment, then shrugged. "Enough about that. Let's get to your first assignment. It's a fitting one for your first day here. I'd like you to find someone for me—and the first one to do it will get bonus marks.

"Find the other visitor in this room."

Gavin froze.

"Identify the other visitor among us, and you get the bonus. You have two days." Kolwezi smiled at the class, and then her gaze fell and was aimed at Gavin. "And good luck!"

• • •

Naturally there was a party every night, or a ball, or ballet or play or re-creation of a famous battle involving tens of thousands of human-shaped bots or real aircraft using real bullets and bombs and built just for the occasion. Such a battle was playing out on the southern horizon right now, choreographed by the famous Nordevns-of-Vientiane. Elana could see flashes of light from the artillery fire. But tonight she was throwing her own event, because Katharine had ordered her to.

She had reviewed the list of invitees with Boto Syre-of-Mbuji-Mayi, the usual Devries party planner. Boto had memorized the constitutions of all the school's students and staff, but even so, the tangled ententes, détentes, pacts, rivalries, and grudges were too complicated for her to include everyone in her class. Within these limitations, Boto had found enough compatible students from other years to make a solid list of a hundred. That was Katharine's minimum for having a good time. Unfortunately, one of them was Jerome Bland-of-Tierra-del-Fuego; to counterbalance him, she'd decided to invite Neal Makhav-of-Winter-Park.

Elana watched gondolas arriving below from the spectacular second-floor gallery that fronted the Grand Canal. The Balashikhas owned a palazzo here called the Fondaco dei Turchi, which should be big enough for a proper party. The palace itself was uncountable thousands of years old, its original builders some family called the Turks. Its ancient marble was lichen-encrusted, but there probably wasn't a stone that hadn't been replaced dozens of times over the centuries. Like the city of Venice itself, the palace was more an idea than a stable object.

Following some other local tradition lost in time, the people disembarking from the gondolas were robed and masked, mostly in simple porcelain ovals painted with exaggerated features. Some faces were framed by giant feathered fans, some costumes billowed or hung oddly, and many of the girls (and some of the boys) wore vast ball gowns that belled out, clearing a meter of space around them.

Elana grunted in satisfaction; she was corseted into such a contraption herself and was relieved she wasn't the only one. She took another look down. The palace's main entrance was on a long portico just a few steps above the waters of the canal. When it was filled with revelers and a queue of full gondolas had built up, she nodded sharply and said, "All right, let them in."

She'd had a trapdoor cut so she could drop straight into the vestibule from the second floor; it would be erased by the morning. As bots opened the vast bronze doors and the crowd tumbled in, she plummeted in on invisible wires, flung her arms out, and shouted, "Welcome!" There was much laughter and whoops of excitement. Still hovering a couple of meters in the air, her own white mask covering her features, she said, "I am Elana Devries-of-Balashikha, your host for tonight. Come in! We have fine food, fine entertainment, and one another. If there's anything more you require, simply ask and it will be yours!"

They poured around her like a flood as she alighted on the floor. *So this is how Katharine does it.* Jugglers and dancers and singing and rousting began—the children of the Million were good at this sort of thing—and she decided to just let it happen. Some of the jugglers and tumblers were bots, but several were human guests, proving the rule of the Million: that no skill or talent ever developed by humanity would not be known by at least one member of each generation. Not just known, but mastered, as Elana had mastered fencing.

The script for the evening started out like clockwork, with music, fine food, diversions, and games. By eight o'clock she had met all her guests and toured them through the palace, losing people here and there to its various distractions. Couples and new friends swirled away and back, ran laughing to and fro. She tried to keep up, but her corset and gown dragged her down, so Elana changed into a tunic and jacket. She kept her mask.

When she came back downstairs she discovered that some of her guests were indolently lounging around watching a movie. They'd chosen an ancient historical epic, *Star Wars*, so one of her main salons was now crammed with sets and lighting gear, plus the full orchestra of bots required to do justice to the score. The movie's characters were running through the audience and fighting with absurd weapons, while in other rooms, storm troopers were being assembled by her house manufacturing unit. A monstrous Death Star was inflating on the roof, and full-scale X-wings and tie fighters, assembled just minutes ago, were starting test flights over the canals.

There was, apparently, a flat-screen-projection version of the story, but naturally no one would be so uncouth as to watch that when they could reproduce the whole thing live.

Still, they could have asked.

Her guests hadn't even told the house bots to stealth the fighter craft, as would have been polite. Two of Elana's neighbors had quick-fabricated antiaircraft batteries on their roofs, and the Empire's squadrons stood a good chance of being shot down before they got a chance to be in the story.

Annoyed, Elana ordered an X-wing to crash into the canal just outside the salon, and when the audience rushed the windows she grabbed a saber, ran into the lounge, and decapitated Luke and Leia. As the audience howled in outrage, she cried, "Catch me if you can!" and led the now properly enlivened guests on a chase through the palace while back in the salon, the *Star Wars* actors and sets quietly dismantled and recycled each other.

Coordinating a party, it seemed, was exhausting in a way that attending one wasn't. Worse, she found she mostly didn't like these people. The character traits that made someone decide to become an auditor were . . . unpleasant. Jerome was typical of them. By nine she found herself back on the gallery, closing the doors behind her and slumping at the balcony for a moment alone. Or—not alone, as a subtle shifting behind her signaled the presence of her minder, the strange, blank-faced bot given her by her class.

She frowned out at the canal and the darkened windows of the city. There were maybe a thousand people crammed into this ancient port, far more than she usually saw together in any one place. In two years all that would change, for one month. Venice would be overrun; the whole world would be.

The partygoers downstairs didn't seem to understand that. Jubilee was almost upon the Million, and during that breach, everything could change.

But there was something else, too, that disquieted her tonight . . .

Somebody coughed, and she stood up straight in surprise. The sound had come from off to her right. A silhouette leaned on the balcony, a good ten meters away. "Who's there?" she called.

"Sorry, is this a private space?" The black cutout on the sky moved, became larger, adopted color and a face; it was one of the boys she'd met at the landing strip. Neal, her counterbalance to Jerome.

"No, I just didn't see you there," she said. He paused,

hesitant, about three meters away.

"Because I would completely understand if you wanted to be alone . . ."

She did, but Katharine would never admit to such an urge, so Elana would not either. "No, it's fine. Are you enjoying the evening?"

"It's a little overwhelming for me," he said, not coming any closer but leaning on the stone balustrade. "I'm from desert country, I'm not used to seeing many people all at the same time."

"Your family doesn't travel much?" She had skimmed his family's constitution, which was very different from hers, but he'd made her party list, so he wasn't that different.

He nodded. "Homebodies, that's us. That is . . . until me." He turned to look at the canal. "It's beautiful here."

"Yes," she said neutrally.

"It's just . . ." He shrugged. "Don't you find this"—he turned, pointed at their two minders, who stood together in the darkness—"a bit odd?"

"Don't you have lots of bots at home?"

"Yes, and I had them discreetly follow me on camping trips when I was younger, that sort of thing. No, it's . . ."

"It's the way everybody's acting around them!"

He nodded. "The older students, from the other classes, they don't have them. But our class does, and everybody's . . . well, downstairs it's as if they're showing off for them."

"I *know!*" She shook her head. "And they're also watching each other, and me, and—"

"Trying to figure out which one of us is the visitor."

"Yeah. When we should be getting to know each other. As friends. It's almost as if the teachers want us to not trust one another . . ." She hadn't realized until she said it that this was what had been bothering her all afternoon. Neal Makhav grunted and leaned out over the canal again.

"Maybe that *is* the lesson," he said. "I was wondering why you threw a masked ball tonight."

"It's a city tradition." But why had she chosen to honor that particular tradition tonight? Once again, she hadn't thought about it until this moment. She turned, paralleling his posture. They both stared at the water. "This isn't what I expected," she said, suddenly miserable.

There was a long silence, punctuated by bursts of music, shouts, splashing, and laughter from downstairs. "I have an idea," Neal said suddenly. She faced him, expectant.

He glanced at their minders, then put his hand aside his mouth and murmured, "Why don't we trade costumes."

Elana laughed in surprise. "What?"

"Shh. Think about it." He moved closer and whispered his next words out at the canal. "Don't you wonder what they're saying about you? And wouldn't it be good to make our shadows, here, work for a change? I'm a little taller, but you could wear heels, and we can swap masks . . ." She gave him a once-over and realized that his jacket and leggings were similar enough to hers that they might even fit. But it would be easier to have a set made; she said so, and he tilted his head from side to side, considering.

"If you can get your tailors to do it without letting *them* know." He nodded back at the shadows.

It was a crazy idea, but the more she thought about it, the better Elana liked it. "I could give the orders in the middle of a dance or—or a sword fight. Do you fence?"

He reared back, laughing. "No! I shoot. Why, do you?"

"Yes. And maybe now's the perfect time to show it off."

They traded a grin and a sharp nod, and went inside.

It went off exactly as Elana hoped: she announced loudly that she would engage in an epee duel with anybody who cared to take her on, and when Jerome stepped up, she made it into an acrobatic affair, leaping on chairs, kicking drinks off tables, and—every time—aiming the mayhem at her minder bot. There was ample opportunity for her to snap an order here and there to her household retinue. By the time she and Jerome declared a draw (with no blood spilled, but much applause), she was on the far side of the mob from her minder and able to duck into an empty corridor where some of her retinue sliced her clothing off her back and others sewed the new suit on without her needing to break stride. She'd seen Neal Makhav duck down another corridor, and she looked for him (now dressed like her) when she reappeared. The plan was not to speak for as long as possible, and keep the minders confused while eavesdropping on the guests. Great fun—though now that she thought about it, just as paranoid as Neal had accused the others of being.

Still, it worked for a while, until the hour passed and she realized that she hadn't seen Neal since she'd donned his appearance.

When she realized this, Elana stopped in mid-dance, swore, and pulled off her mask. "Wait a sec—"

But by then, of course, it was far too late. She'd been played.

• • •

Gavin looked back. There was no sign of his shadow anywhere.

He'd thought about using the canals, but even if he were submerged and invisible, they were a slow way to get around. He and Bernie used to use jumpers—simple back-mounted fans that couldn't really let you fly but generated just enough lift to enable you to jump prodigious distances. He'd spotted one in the zeppelin and had passed a written note to one of his bots to have it cached near Elana's palace. After tricking her into changing costumes, it had been an easy thing to find it, put it on, and jump away across the Grand Canal.

Like his gambit at the aircar, tonight's attempt to ditch his shadow was a long shot. He didn't know how persistent a follower the bot was, but he couldn't take any chances. If Destiny Kolwezi already knew he was a visitor, then Karelia had betrayed him or . . . Eli had or, or *something.* He didn't know what had happened, only that he must have been exposed somehow. When Elana had announced her party and said that it would be a costume ball, he'd seen a chance to play a trick on his minder. He was pretty sure he wouldn't get another chance.

He ran toward the edge of the roof and leaped into the dark air. Instantly, the jumper's fan kicked in, lofting him over the black abyss of an alley.

He had an important errand to run tonight, and it wasn't for Eli Makhav.

• • •

Two masked figures stepped in front of Elana as she was

trotting down the stone steps to a waiting gondola—her shadow not far behind. "Um . . . say . . . are you leaving your own party?" said the shorter one in Hemandar's voice.

"It's a costume ball! No one will notice. Cover for me, will you?"

"But . . ." The gondolier cast off and she and her robotic stalker sat awkwardly across from each other as they slipped into the canal.

"It's not you, it's me," she said to her shadow. It didn't reply.

"It's never going to work. We're too different."

Still nothing. "Oh, forget it." Not five minutes ago, she had spotted another shadow moving through the palace, clearly searching for someone. It was Neal Makhav's, she was sure of it. He'd used her to ditch it. She was going to find out why.

• • •

The auditors' prison had once been some sort of religious building, with a tall spire and walls that were curtains of colored glass. It was cross-shaped and, despite its airy appearance, had only three entrances. These were well watched from ground level by security bots armed with stun guns, tanglers, and sound cannon.

Gavin had come in via the roof.

The place was mostly one big room, sumptuously decorated with couches, workstations for any kind of craft one might want to indulge in, and a stage with actor fakes currently sitting tilted like abandoned dolls. There was a massive kitchen, string quartet (also idle), and many other distractions and amenities. Bernie sat in a plain chair beneath the vast round window at one end of the main aisle, reading.

But not alone. Six alert military bots stood at attention, three facing him, three looking out. There was no way Gavin was just going to walk up to Bernie unnoticed. Luckily, he'd anticipated this.

When he was seven, Gavin had learned how to make an annoying clicking sound with his tongue. He'd spent weeks following Bernie around, clicking at him. To this day, if he wanted to send his brother into high alert, all he needed to do was make one click.

First, he found a position between the stage and the above-floor hot tub where he could see Bernie but not the bots. He made one click, aiming it into the rafters. Then, from his position in the shadows, he watched as the tiny sound echoed around the chamber.

Bernie sat up suddenly and looked around himself. When his eyes tracked in Gavin's direction, Gavin made a slow wave with one hand.

Bernie froze, opened his mouth, and looked around. The bots. Gavin nodded, but stuck his hands out in front of him, shook them in the air once, then formed the shapes their father had taught the boys to use for long-distance signaling when they were hunting. He'd called it *sign language.*

How are you? he asked Bernie. There was a bruise on his brother's forehead and his knuckles were skinned and swollen. *Did they hurt you?*

Bernie grimaced. *I attacked these.* He nodded at the out-of-sight guardbots. *They just stood there.*

Gavin nodded. Bernie would have gotten angry. He'd lash out; he couldn't help himself. But he would never try to hurt anything living.

I've come to get you out.

Bernie stared at him for a moment, then chuckled and shook his head. *You and what army?*

Gavin looked away, stomach knotting. He'd thought about it. Neal Makhav had resources, he could have ordered up a military force like any other kid. He might even get Bernie out of this building with it. Whatever he threw at the situation, the auditors could do a hundred times more. So he shook his head. *I don't know. Stealth. We have no time! They're on to me.*

Eli Makhav?

He knows, but he says he doesn't care. No, it's the auditors.

You're sure?

The question hung there. As the seconds stretched, Bernie shook his head. *Let them prove it by arresting you. Otherwise, we win in trial and go home together.*

Gavin tried to smile, to nod yes to this, but he couldn't pretend. *Eli Makhav wants me to keep playing Neal Makhav.*

Why?

He spread his hands helplessly. He hoped the expression on his face would communicate how he felt. *Bernie, what do I do?*

He expected Bernie to lose focus or burst into one of his rages. Instead, the smile that lit up his face brought to the surface a Bernard Penn that Gavin hadn't seen since the accident.

You'll think of something. I trust you. Gavin felt a flush of embarrassed pride.

He turned to go, but something had been nagging at him, and he couldn't ignore it. Gavin didn't know when he would see his brother again—or if. Reluctantly, he looked Bernie in the eye and signed, *What was Plan B?*

Bernie looked away. Some complex emotion troubled his face. When he met Gavin's gaze again, it was with obvious difficulty.

It was my idea. If I couldn't be . . . fixed . . . we could alter your face to make you look like me. And send you out into the world. You could have a life, get married, have friends—

Bernie broke off, crossing his arms and stuffing his hands under them. It took a long time before he looked up again.

Gavin hadn't moved; he couldn't, until he could look Bernie in the eye again.

I love you, Brother, he signed. *I will get you out.*

Then he turned and crept away.

• • •

Elana could have summoned a thousand camera drones from the family aerostat, which still hung over Venice like a delirious moon. But that would have alerted—and maybe alarmed—the auditors, who had their own surveillance networks and armies sleeping in bunkers that she dared not wake. In addition, her family's treaty with the Makhavs forbade such overt espionage.

"Damn the treaties," she muttered now as she hung upside down from a grappling hook precariously dug into the lip of Neal Makhav's roof. In ancient times there had been something called Law, which applied equally to everybody; supposedly, the locksteppers still used it. Of course you'd have to, in a primitive state where the ideal of civilization was the anthill. But laws wouldn't do in a world where each person had his or her own economy, complete with factories, and each family ran an estate the size of an ancient country. So the Million took out treaties with one another, drew mutual lines they agreed not to cross, declared certain behaviors unacceptable. There was no grand treaty that held for everyone. The placeholder for that was their treaties with the lockstep, which were all identical.

"Thou shall not overpopulate in our absence," she grated, to keep her mind on something other than the drop to the icy waters of the canal. She'd climbed like this before; most kids practiced all manner of dangerous stunts, and Elana was no exception. "You must repair or rebuild our dwellings should they deteriorate while we sleep . . ." The list went on. It added up to a set of obligations that often made the Million feel like the lockstep's janitors.

She inched her way a little closer to the lighted window she'd spotted from above. She could hear voices. Frustrated, she let out more line and overshot, nearly losing her grip. Swearing under her breath, she grabbed for the windowsill, had it for a moment, then let go, twirling. She swung aside the wall like a pendulum, and only at the midpoint of the swing could she make out what the people in the room were saying.

"What do you mean, they know?" It was an older man, the voice was deep and authoritative. "They can't!"

"They can and they do." That was Neal Makhav. "And

not so loud. *It* is listening."

Now Elana was past, and the voices were mumbles. When she swung back it was in time to hear Neal say, in a puzzled tone, "What do you mean, they're not looking for me? How do you know that?" That was all she got before she was past again.

She had to stop this swinging, if only because the twirling was making her stomach churn. Elana stretched out her arm to drag her fingers along the plaster face of the building.

"Oh, do sit down," the older man was saying. "You look like you're about to faint."

"But who—"

"I can't tell you that. That would be cheating." Elana snatched her arm back as she passed the window, then dragged her fingers again. This seemed to work; she was able to grab the windowsill on the way back and hang there under it.

"Now listen up, I have a job for you. I can't have you all panicky about your classmates, so put all of that nonsense out of your head.

"I want you to mug the auditors' Archive and steal a file for me. Yes, yes, the Archive's not a place, it's a thing, it looks like one of the footmen. You just need to get it alone and make sure it doesn't recognize your face or voice. Now listen, here's the filename I want, and the password to calm down the Archive . . ."

Elana felt a thrill of triumph. She'd found the class's visitor! She couldn't wait to stand up tall tomorrow and declare what she'd learned. Meanwhile, though, what was all this about breaking into an archive?

"But how do I find this Archive bot?" asked Neal, sounding tired and peevish.

"How the hell should I know, you're the one who's there. I need it in the next two days." He rattled off a document name and some account information; Elana cursed the treaties for forbidding her to use recording equipment around a Makhav. She whispered the instructions to herself, desperate to remember them. "Memorize that, don't write it down," the older man was saying. "And for the ancestors' sake, stop acting sneaky around that bot. I swear, you're your own worst enemy."

Elana risked bracing her feet against the wall and creeping up to look over the windowsill. Gavin stood before an animated statue. Obviously angry, he looked up at the ornate ceiling, then at the telepresence bot.

"My own worst enemy?" he said slowly. "No, I'm pretty sure that's you."

The statue grinned. "Two days," it said as it turned to climb onto a marble pedestal. "And mind you, don't neglect your studies. I'll be watching." It struck a heroic pose and froze in place.

For a moment there was only the quiet sound of water lapping and distant music from the party down the canal. Neal Makhav stood as frozen as the statue. Then Elana's hand slipped. "Ack!"

"What—?" He was going to find her! She couldn't climb back up in time . . . which left one option.

Elana closed her eyes and unclipped herself from her line.

• • •

Early the next day, one of the teachers' bots dropped by to inform Elana that this morning's class would be taking place on the shores of an Indonesian island. Suborbital rockets were waiting on the landing field—"One per student," the bot said primly. Elana, halfway down the vast marble staircase, blew out her cheeks in annoyance. School was fast becoming a relentlessly tedious experience.

She reached the landing field to find five rockets remaining, and the dwindling contrails of a dozen others arrowed straight into the zenith. She clambered into one, saying grumpily, "Oh, you wouldn't miss this for the world, would you?" when her shadow climbed in after her. She was favoring the shoulder she had landed on when she hit the water last night.

What she hated the most was that this faceless, voiceless machine had been the one to fish her out of the canal when she'd struggled, all breath gone and stung from impact, two meters into the black depths. She refused to thank it.

There was little to do while the rocket flattened her into her acceleration bed but watch the shadow sit unmoving as though nothing were happening. The Million refused any virtual experiences, so there was no hiding behind VR goggles or augmented reality as the crass Ancients or the modern locksteppers might do. She was reduced to staring out the window at the curve of Earth's horizon as she arced over it, from dawn to late afternoon in fifteen minutes.

This morning's class turned out to consist of watching some senior auditors clean up a spill on an otherwise perfect white beach. Haixi Bang lectured the class on the situation, his backdrop a million tonnes of gold bursting from the split side of a rust-red cargo pod the size of a skyscraper. The asteroid-mining pod had hit hard and half buried itself in the sand. Torched palm trees stuck up like withered hairs from a blackened landscape that was still smoking despite the circling fire-suppressant drones.

The Indonesians, all twenty-four of them, had come out to complain. Professor Haixi spent much of the morning reassuring them that this would never happen again.

Of course the Million weren't alone in the solar system; there were other civilizations out there, some of them vast, not all of them human. Still, Elana agreed with the Indonesians: this was *their* land. Any incursion, however accidental, was deeply insulting.

The rest of the class seemed to agree, except for Neal Makhav, whose expression when he looked at the cargo container was oddly wistful.

As lunchtime approached, Destiny Kolwezi summoned everyone to a sumptuously appointed barge in the middle of the bay (design by Lem-of-Carpentaria), and when they had settled, she said, "Any progress on yesterday's assignment?"

This was her chance. Elana leaped to her feet. "I know who it is!"

Kolwezi crossed her arms, squinting at Elana. "Do you now?"

"It's him! Neal Makhav! I followed him last night, heard him talking to—"

Makhav jumped to his feet, a panicked look on his face, and rightly so, thought Elana, yet Kolwezi was saying something. "What, ma'am? I'm sorry, I didn't—"

"I said, Devries, do you have proof of this allegation?" Kolwezi's frown was severe.

"Pr-oooff." Elana tasted the unfamiliar syllables. "Um, no. You see, the treaties—that is, the Makhav and Devries treaties, they forbid—"

Now Kolwezi smiled. "Without proof I'm afraid your allegation will remain just that. And I believe you've just rendered a deep insult to Mr. Makhav. According to the Devries and Makhav treaties, he might even be within his rights to challenge you to a duel over it."

"Bu-but it's him, I—"

"No, it's not him, we all know who it is!" Jerome Bland-of-Tierra-del-Fuego stood, hands on his hips, and sneered at Elana. "She broke down and admitted it at your party last night. And where were you? Oh! Now I get it!" He turned, raising his arms like a conductor to the class. "Stalk-ing! Neal! Makhav!"

A huge burst of laughter swarmed Elana. She felt her insides curling up, and knew she was flushing.

"But he really—he—"

"Violetta Mimieux-of-Alsace is the visitor," snapped Jerome, dismissing Elana with a wave. "She's a lockstep-per, on loan for a term while she studies to become a lockstep auditor. Everybody knew it by this morning. Everybody but you."

The whole class laughed. Again.

Elana sat down quickly. A bot offered her an icy glass of something orange, and she had to resist the urge to punch it. "I retract my allegation," she said tightly.

Violetta Mimieux had been born in the lockstep, Elana

learned. She was seventeen years old, meaning that she had experienced seventeen years of life. In fact, she had been born six thousand years ago. After her season in Venice, she would be returning to the lockstep, which meant Elana might see her again, in two years, and then not for another thirty—at which time she would not yet have turned eighteen. She seemed comfortable with the idea that, by the time she graduated and became an auditor, everyone now sitting around her would have been dead for centuries.

Kolwezi began to talk about the strange implications of the time difference between lockstep and Million, but Elana wasn't listening. She felt a gaze burning into the back of her head, and knew that if she turned around, all she would see was Neal Makhav's look of hurt betrayal.

• • •

Gavin watched a flight of hypersonics lift off from the piazza in front of the Doge's Palace. Half his class were heading off to some other continent to party until the wee hours.

He'd been out walking, restless in his unfamiliar apartments. As evening light fell like a shower of rose petals, the streets and canals filled with cheerful people, but he felt separate from them, as if he were still dancing with bots next door to the real ballroom with its real people. He wanted to smile and say hello to someone, but the people he passed were wrapped up in each other. They were mannered and perfect, like all the Million. Compared to them, he felt like a shambling bear from the back country.

Every morning he woke with a start, sure that it was 3 a.m., that a bot was shaking his shoulder and telling him he must rise and flee. The peaceful call of morning birds, the singing of gondoliers (historical specialists all, as rich as any Million) could not convince him otherwise. He needed to get up, walk, shower, and clear his head. When he did, he would inevitably pass the baleful statue of Eli Makhav, and his shoulders would hunch every time. The palace was not his home, so tonight, like all nights, he would stay away from it until exhaustion drove him back. Luckily today, Eli had no assignment for him.

"Well, good evening, Neal!"

It took him a full second to remember that Neal was supposed to be his name. Blinking, Gavin turned to find Destiny Kolwezi smiling at him from the pool of shadow beneath an archway. He bowed. "Good evening, Master."

She laughed lightly. "We're not in class right now, Neal, you can call me Destiny." He nodded stiffly as she emerged from the darkness. "On your way to a friend's? Or returning?"

"Ah . . . returning." He made a vague gesture in the direction he'd been going, but his palace was behind him.

Kolwezi began walking in the direction he'd been going, and politeness demanded that he fall in step beside her. Her expression was musing, a bit crafty as it often was, and now she said, "And who were you visiting? It seems to me that you're a bit of a man apart. But then, I only ever see you in class."

And always at the back, or in a corner, or otherwise disengaged, he knew. But what could he do about that? He shrugged.

"Then again, I hear you're quite the trickster," she continued. "They say you pranked Elana Devries-of-Balashikha at her own party. Is she still mad at you?"

"I . . . I don't know—"

"—Because you haven't talked to her since." Kolwezi frowned and shook her head. They were walking along a canal now, its dark waters a lapping invisible presence. "You weren't planning to apologize?"

"She accused me of being a visitor." The fact was it actually hadn't occurred to him. When not trying to keep up with his classmates, or evading his shadow so he could spy on the auditors, Gavin thought only about Bernie. His head was full of plans to break his brother out, or implicate Karelia somehow in the death of their father. But he couldn't say this to Kolwezi.

Still, she nodded. "I know what it's like to be the stranger in a strange land. I was the outsider once—I would say, much more than you, but then I don't really know you. Still, I've been watching you, Neal, and I wince every now and then." She grinned. "I almost see myself sitting there, not meeting anyone's eyes or hurrying away after class without chatting with anyone. That's a puzzle, because you seem so fierce and self-assured when you've got a plan."

"Oh." He had no idea how to answer that.

Kolwezi laughed again. "Apologize to the girl. Consider it an assignment."

He began to stammer a thanks, but she had already vanished into the shadows. And when he looked around to find her, he realized that the light he stood in came from the windows of the palace of Elana Devries-of-Balashikha.

"Apologize, apologize," he muttered as he snuck up on, rather than walked to, the entrance. He was trying to remember proper etiquette around *apologies*. Bernie and he hadn't needed them; they would fight, there would be a winner and a loser, and next day all would be forgotten. He was sure Elana wasn't like that—though, now that he thought about it, she *was* a fencing champion . . .

What would Bernie—the old Bernie, whom Gavin remembered with reverence bordering on awe—have done? Actually, it was obvious what Bernie would have done. Realizing that, Gavin had an extra thought: maybe Kolwezi was right about him being more confident when he had a plan. Terrifying as that first party at Elana's had been, he'd remained calm and even managed to trick her and her shadow.

Now he strode up to the door and rapped smartly on it, refusing to second-guess himself.

A bot in Devries livery opened the door. "Good evening, Mr. Makhav. Are you expected?"

"No. No, I'm not. Can you tell Elana I'd like to see her?"

"Yes, sir." It bowed and shut the door—and then, waiting, Gavin's heart began to pound.

Several long minutes passed, then the door swung back to reveal Elana, dressed in fencing gear. Gavin felt wobbly, but he bowed.

"I think we got off on the wrong foot," he said. "I was hoping to make up for it."

"So you've come to apologize? You made a fool of me at my own party." But she quirked a smile as she said this.

"Technically, I tricked my shadow into thinking you were me. That's different." He ventured a grin, cautious the way he was with Bernie after a fight. "Anyway, you accused me of being a visitor in front of everybody! So maybe it's you who should apologize to me."

She still looked amused. "You seriously expect me to do that? Come in, by the way."

"You were fencing?" They made their way through the statue-filled, marble-and-amber-paneled front hall. "I'll tell you what. Let's duel. The loser apologizes to the winner, and then no more hard feelings?"

She turned, tapping a finger on her cheek, smiling past it at him. "Who gets choice of weapons?"

"You're going to choose swords, aren't you?" he said resignedly.

"Why, yes, I think I am." She laughed and clapped her hands. "We need gear for Mr. Makhav! And a good epee."

"Epee? Not foil?" He was decent with foil and had expected that to be her weapon. Epee was heavier, more a man's sport. Or so he thought.

She made short work of him. "Oh, but that wasn't fair, was it?" she said after. "Go again?" Guardedly, he nodded. She humiliated him again. And then again. Frustrated, she said, "Why are you letting me do this to you?"

He shrugged. "You don't think I deserve it?"

"Yes. Yes! I do! Again!" After ten minutes and almost twenty disarmaments, mortal threats, and formal losses, Elana threw down her epee and shouted, "Bah! You're done! Admit you were wrong."

Gavin dropped his own sword, went down on one

knee, and said, "Elana Devries-of-Balashikha, can you forgive me for playing a trick on you at your own party?"

"Oh, no. Not at all." She flipped off her mask and strode for the door to an inner parlor. Gavin shot after her.

"But we agreed! The loser would apologize and—"

"And what? I didn't agree that the winner would have to *accept* that apology."

He sputtered for a second—Bernie had never done anything like this!—then found himself laughing again. He bowed. "I'll take my leave, then."

"Oh, stop it!" She grabbed his arm and dragged him into the parlor, with three bots and two shadows jamming the doorway behind them. "Neal, I swear, you're so formal you practically speak in verse! Sit down and have a snack. I'm just dying to complain to somebody about Bang's latest assignment . . ."

So he sat, and they talked, and it was strange, and utterly new and wonderful. For the first time since that terrible night when the house burned, Gavin forgot revenge and the need to rescue Bernie. Though he would feel guilty about it later, in this moment, and for the very first time in his life, he felt himself in the presence of a friend.

• • •

Having friends might be wonderful, but it had never occurred to Gavin that it might also make his investigation easier.

Eli wanted to know everything that was going on in Venice, and so far, Gavin had been finding out by skulking, eavesdropping, and sending bots to watch the comings and goings of auditors, teachers, and other bots. Eli was particularly interested in Karelia and his friends, an interest Gavin shared. His shadow witnessed all of these investigations, of course, but Gavin had concluded it would never tell on him. It watched him for other reasons.

With Elana to talk to, though, he'd discovered that if he wondered something about the personal or private affairs of any of the auditors, all he had to do was *ask*. She seemed as intensely interested in the auditors' power structure as he was—almost more so, which was weird.

Hemandar Satna appeared to have adopted Gavin as well. Hemandar was a builder, obsessed with his designs, but he knew everything about bots and other technical systems.

Ross Donegal remained standoffish, but he kept up with gossip, so Gavin worked at becoming his friend. Now that he wasn't surrounded by his shield of fakes, Ross turned out to be charming, if sarcastic. Gossip was king in Venice, and only now was Gavin beginning to understand that his own standoffishness had given rise to many rumors and suspicions about him. He was quick to deflate them, though every now and then he saw a certain reserve in Elana's eyes. She knew *something,* he just didn't know what, and of all things, he was afraid to ask about that.

While all this was going on, he also saw more of the world over the next few weeks than he had in his entire life.

It was perfectly normal for Destiny Kolwezi to stroll into class and say, "Pair up, we're flying to Peru to look at the ecosystem effects of human communities," or, "There's a lifter waiting outside. Today we're exploring an abandoned lockstep fortress in Antarctica."

Tony Cupun built mock towns and hid bots in them; the students had to play hide-and-seek with the targets while other bots sniped at them from rooftops. He simulated a rebellious Great House by manufacturing an entire bot army, and made the class go to war against it. (The epic battles took place on the back side of the moon, where the nuclear explosions and indiscriminate laser fire wouldn't be noticeable from Earth.)

Gavin had played with armies before, when he and Bernie ran riot across the Chaffee hills. But Dad (Martin Penn, he had to remind himself) had never let them go all out with their games. The auditors did.

Once, in central Asia, the class became separated in a dust storm while battling mechs. Gavin had seen storms like this back home and pushed doggedly through it, his shadow silently following, until he spotted two figures huddled behind a gnarled stump. It was Ross Donegal and his own shadow. In the whipping wind, Ross looked lost and terrified; vague giant shapes stomped about in the distance, while bullets whined and stuff exploded. Gavin stalked up to the stump, silently held out his hand, and pulled Ross to his feet. They went on together, and after that much of Ross's sharpness toward Gavin vanished.

Classes back in Venice might have seemed dull and boring by comparison, were it not for Kolwezi's uncomfortable moral dilemmas, and Haixi Bang's intellectual puzzles.

One day, Kolwezi singled out Ross for her relentless questions. "Donegal, how can you believe we're anything more than the lockstep's janitors? Aren't we here just to sweep out their houses while they're away?" They'd been talking about the great museum cities, like Paris and Beijing, that the Million tended so diligently. Common wisdom had it that these were the Million's property, rented out for one month every thirty years to the tumultuous rabble of the lockstep.

Ross crossed his arms, arched an eyebrow, and said, "We're equals! How else do you explain the treaties?" Haixi Bang had been drilling those relentlessly into their heads over the past week. There were three kinds of treaty: those between the Great Families, those between the Million and the ecological AIs that presided over Earth's biophysical health; and the ancient, grand treaty with the lockstep. There were only a few rules common to all treaties, such as the Millions' universal refusal to allow their artificial intelligences to network in any way. Both the Million and the lockstep had auditors to enforce their terms. The eco-AIs had . . . other things.

"If the locksteppers controlled the whole planet," Ross continued, "they could have bots maintain their cities and grow their food. That's how it works on most lockstep worlds, right? There's no Million on Mars, the whole place is silent as a tomb right now—well, except for the Tharks. Anyway, they don't automate what we do, because they can't! The Million are here because we refused to give the whole planet over to the lockstep. And there are one Million of us because that's all the humans Earth's ecosystem can handle. I mean, day to day."

Kolwezi adopted a sly look. "Then, if we're so independent, why do we still speak the same language as the locksteppers? Have similar names? Similar culture? We've been separate from them for thousands and thousands of years. Wouldn't we drift apart?"

Ross looked like he'd swallowed a whole pineapple. He was visibly struggling to reply when Dean Tuyuc-of-Cuzco appeared at the side door. "Professor Kolwezi, could you spare a moment for a couple of announcements?"

Kolwezi bowed to her. It wasn't unusual for the dean to drop by; personal visits were polite, distant PA announcements rude. "Of course, Dean. Class?"

They all stood and bowed as well. Tuyuc-of-Cuzco walked to the center of the stage and put her hands on her hips. "I have two announcements," she said, her voice easily carrying to the back of the hall. "The first is this: the shadow tests are about to start.

"Remember, these are hide-and-seek exercises. You and your shadow have had all term to get to know each other. Now it's time to use that knowledge. For the first test, you will be required to evade your minder and hide, for no less than two days. You may do this at any time in the next month. You can go to ground anywhere on the planet during that time and are not required to report your absence or whereabouts to the school. If you are unable to get away from your shadow, or are caught within the first two days, you fail the test. After that, the roles are reversed. Your shadow will hide from you, with similar conditions. I wish you the best of luck; to succeed you'll have to apply all the skills and knowledge we've taught you.

"Second, for those interested, the schedule for the murder trial of Bernard Penn has been moved up. It will begin in two days. Bernard Penn-of-Chaffee is accused in the death of his father; I'm sure most of you have heard the stories by now. Any student who wishes to skip classes to attend the trial is free to do so, as long as you notify your teachers. Just bear in mind that seating is limited, so be there early." She bowed. "That is all."

Gavin sat numbly for the rest of the class, missing everything Kolwezi said. He felt like a heavy lid had slammed down on him, cutting off his tentative feeling of belonging. The room around him was once again full of strangers.

As the students erupted from their seats after class, they burst into chatter and speculation—mostly about the shadow tests but also about the murder trial. Gavin heard Bernie described as a remorseless, shambling half human, a brain-damaged idiot, and a cunning manipulator only pretending to be disabled. He shouldered his way through the crowd, books clutched to his chest, spilling with the others into the fresh air of the courtyard. All he wanted was to go home.

". . . just found out!" Elana was saying brightly to a small crowd. "Of course, Tatiana's one of the best trial lawyers, but that she should be the defense for this case . . . well, I'll definitely be attending." Gavin stumbled and stopped.

"Shame she's the defender, though," drawled Jerome

Bland. "Won't look good on her, taking the side of a homicidal lunatic. She's bound to lose, mmm?"

"Your aunt's defending Bernie?" blurted Gavin. All heads turned.

Elana crossed her arms and narrowed her eyes. "Bernard Penn, yes," she said.

Gavin grabbed her arm and hauled her away from the others. "I have to talk to you," he said. "I mean, I have to talk to *her.*"

"What? Why?"

"I know Bernie. I know him, and, and . . . I was there."

Elana's eyes went wide, and she twisted out of his grip. "What are you saying? You saw the murder?"

Gavin knew he was throwing away any pretense of investigating on his own, even of being a student here. What choice did he have? The only reason he'd gone on with this charade was to buy time while finding a way to save Bernie. He hadn't found any such way, and the trial was coming. There was only one option left.

"Listen, just tell her I want to talk to her. Can you get me in to see her? Before the trial, I mean. I have . . . I have important information." Even now he held on to a slim hope that he could invent a lie plausible enough to both save Bernie and his own pretend-life as Neal Makhav. Eli might help with that . . . but Elana was shaking her head.

Not in denial, apparently, but alarm. "Is this why . . .

I think I get it now. Neal, is this why you came to the school? Because of Bernard—Bernie?"

He shrugged, looked away. "Just tell her, please! Can you do that for me? And don't tell anybody else?"

She nodded, but as Gavin walked away, he thought about where they were. Looking up, the empty windows surrounding the auditors' school seemed to be staring back.

• • •

Gavin felt meditative and calm as he prepared for the meeting. The auditor candidates had a school uniform, gray as opposed to the stark black of the professionals. The Million seldom wore uniforms; some of them didn't wear clothing at all. Gavin knew the sameness of the apparel was meant to make people uneasy, and it did. It made him uneasy to wear it. So he laid it aside and let the bots sew him into a set of tough traveling gear, like he and Bernie wore when they went out on the land for a few days.

He didn't mind leaving behind the Million, for he had no ties to them other than Bernie. The people at the school . . . Ross and Hemandar could be friends, but Gavin didn't really know what having friends felt like, so he couldn't be sure. Elana? *She knows something about me she's not saying,* he reminded himself.

"Sir?" said one of the sewing bots.

"Nothing. Go on." He raised his chin and stared at the wall.

The hardest thing about exile to the lockstep would be plummeting forward into the future, thirty years every month. You would always know that any fox you met on a path, or bird you saw wheeling in the sky would be long dead the next time you walked this way. To enter a lockstep was to leave ordinary time behind. The claim was that in return he would gain the stars, but Gavin had no interest in the stars. It was the lives of the wildlife of Chaffee that he had always cared about.

Somberly, he sized himself up in the mirror. Visible in the reflection was his shadow, standing three meters behind him as always. "You'll love this," he said to it. "All right." He turned to one of the household bots. "Get me a ballistic shuttle or a helicopter or something. I'm going to the Devries estate."

"Very good, sir." The bot gestured to two others, and another opened the French doors. Gavin stalked past them and down the hall to an elevator, where two more beckoned. His thoughts were on his accusation against Karelia, and what Tatiana Devries might do with it. How the judge would react and how long it would take for his cover story to fall apart. Distracted as he was, he didn't notice that the elevator was going down instead of up—and very quickly—until they stopped with a sharp jerk. "Is there a hangar down here?"

"No, Mr. Makhav."

Gavin snapped to attention. "Where's my shadow?" Two of his household bots flanked him, and a third stood behind him. When the elevator doors opened, a blast of icy air chased all the warmth out of the car. Outside was darkness, dim specks of light, and a strange absence of echo that implied some huge space.

Hesitantly, Gavin stepped out. "What is this place?"

Another bot stepped into view outside the elevator. "We misdirected your shadow with a fake of yourself, sir. Our apologies. As to this place—"

"Lockstep!"

He stood near the top of a huge domed cavern. The stone ceiling that curved down to become wall was reinforced with a honeycomb of giant metal triangles, lit here and there by tiny pinprick lights. This ersatz sky overhung a cityscape whose buildings were machines, whose avenues led to and from countless stacks that, from here, looked like bookshelves. Only it wasn't books jammed into those distant shelves but the frost-painted sides of the legendary cicada beds—each containing a frozen man, woman, or child.

Gavin shivered and, in a flash, felt a terrible déjà vu, as

if he'd stood here before, staring at these same shelved crowds. He remembered feeling this same confusion and fear.

He spun, looking back at the elevator, which he now saw was the terminus of a new-looking metal shaft that penetrated the ceiling. "Shadow—?"

"By the time it entered the hallway," said the bot beside him, "the elevator doors were gone, and within an hour the shaft itself will have been silently renovated out of the building."

The elevator doors *had* been in a funny place, not the wall where he usually found them, but that sort of change happened all the time back home. He had been too distracted to notice.

"You're not Makhav bots," he said. "You spoofed the household help, too." Doing that was a treaty violation. Just building bots that were capable of it could get you a visit from the auditors . . .

. . . which meant, of course, that nobody understood how to do something like this better than the auditors themselves. He knew who was behind it.

"Follow me, sir, your apartments are this way." The bot said nothing more, simply gestured patiently. With a last sigh and look at the elevator, Gavin did what he was told.

• • •

". . . and in all the time you've known Bernard, did you ever see him act violently toward his father?"

"Well . . ." Lidetta Fance-of-Burgundy looked up, down, at the judge, and everywhere but at the prosecutor who'd asked the question. "Never before the accident. After . . . you see, you must understand, Bernie would never hurt a rabbit. He was the kindest soul . . ." She seemed on the verge of tears.

"Can you answer the question, please?"

"Yes, but no! Yes, he was violent, but he couldn't help himself! He didn't plan it! He wasn't angry, never angry with anyone, he—"

"Thank you. And on the evening of the incident, did you see him act violently toward Martin Penn?"

As the silence stretched, Tatiana Devries-of-Balashikha twisted in her seat to look up at Elana. Elana shrugged and shook her head. No, she hadn't been able to find any sign of Neal Makhav during the court's last break. Tatiana scowled and turned back to the unfolding fiasco.

Neal hadn't been in class yesterday, yet it wasn't until late afternoon that a Devries courier had come to find Elana. Aunt Tatiana was concerned: Elana had told her that Neal had last-minute information for the defense, yet he hadn't shown up for the meeting he himself had demanded.

Elana had been hunting for him ever since.

The prosecution seemed just as put out by his absence; there'd been some hurried discussion with the judge, and now testimony was being called from character witnesses. Actual recounting of the events surrounding Martin Penn's death would have to wait.

The prosecution was painting Bernie as a psychopath prone to delusions and unpredictable rages. His original statement had involved an elaborate story about having a secret visitor brother, whom Neal Makhav supposedly murdered. He'd since retracted the story, but he gave no reason for why he'd told it in the first place. That was not putting his sanity in a good light.

The Million's Treaty Resolution Board had flown in a tall, open-ceilinged round theater to house the trial. (The Crales-of-Manhattan were apparently outraged that they hadn't been commissioned to design and build one especially for the occasion.) Tens of thousands of years old, originally from Britain or somewhere, the theater had been scooped up delicately by an aerostat bigger than the Devrieses' and gently deposited on a custom-built raft in the waters just outside the Doge's Palace. The Crales had been asked to design the footbridge that led to it; they weren't appeased by this token gesture.

Witnesses and court officials sat on benches on the main floor of the ancient building, with the judge, jury, and dock on the stage. The three rings of seating rising above this were packed with visitors, some of whom Elana recognized.

On the benches, waiting to testify, were Thomas Jagand-of-Karelia, other guests who'd been at the party, and a man who closely resembled the marble statue in Neal Makhav's foyer.

Elana had been watching this man. Much of his attention was fixed on Karelia; every now and then, however, he glanced up at a particular spot in the gallery. It had taken Elana much time and estimation to figure out where he was looking. Now she impatiently waited for the next recess to confirm her suspicions.

As soon as the judge announced a break, Elana grabbed a member of her retinue and hauled it through the milling crowd until she spotted the group she was looking for. "There!" She pointed. "Who are those people?"

The bot peered through the forest of perfumed, elaborately costumed Million, Thousand, and Hundred. "I believe you are asking about Antonin Vera-of-Almaty and family. They live in central Asia."

"Okay. So, why are *they* watching them like hawks?" She pointed at Eli Makhav, who was nearby, arguing heatedly with Destiny Kolwezi.

Elana had seen them together this morning and thought it must be a coincidence. But now her bot said, "I do not know, ma'am. However, the Veras have been tentatively chosen as the replacement for the Penn family as stewards of Chaffee, should Bernard Penn be found unfit to take on his role as head of that household."

"Oh? Oh!"

She took another look around. Nobody was paying any attention to her.

"Gather the rest of our people," she told the bot. "We have another appointment today."

• • •

"Wait, wait!" Ross paced back and forth, nervously watching Elana's guards, who stood on all the nearby rooftops. "This whole school term, you've been *spying on* the auditors?"

"Not spying. Investigating. Citizen journalism." That was a very old term she'd dug up in the library. Nowadays most journalism was gossip amplification, but there were a few respected writers. The Fourth Estate was one of those institutions the Million prided itself in preserving, so Ross should get the reference.

Ross and Hemandar knew Neal better than anybody else, and she liked them both, so she'd pulled them out of class. They were happy to sneak away and expected her to update them on the progress of the trial. Neither had been awake early enough to get in. Once she had them, though, she'd hustled them out of the Doge's Palace and brought them here.

There was no way she was going to have this conversation at home, and they might have been spotted flying up to the family aerostat. Elana had walked the boys to an ancient courtyard about a kilometer from the Doge's Palace. It was beautiful, a single gnarled tree presiding over a square pool in its center. Nobody ever came here. She'd summoned a security detail, which had taken up posts in all the alleys, nearby buildings, and rooms and stairwells of the empty mansions. This courtyard was, for the moment at least, Devries territory.

"I'm not spying," she repeated. "Some of the Hundred are concerned about the integrity of the auditors. I've been investigating, yes. And why shouldn't I?"

"Oh, no, no, that's just"—Ross struggled to find a word—"amazing! But how can you do that—how can we even have this conversation—with them?" He nodded at their shadows.

Elana's guard detail was keeping them behind a low wall about fifty meters away. Other bots were holding up large fans to obscure Elana, Ross, and Hemandar's heads from the shadows' line of sight. "If those things have better-than-human senses and are listening in right now, then they're massively violating our treaties.

And if they've gone that far, we're in way deeper trouble than I thought. For a while I tried to investigate without raising my own's suspicions"—she nodded at her shadow—"but it was just too hard, and anyway, it's supposed to have a vow of silence about all our activities. I checked. It would be another treaty violation if it reported any of the stuff I've been up to."

"So what have you found out?" Hemandar asked eagerly. He seemed to be taking this revelation more calmly than Ross.

"Not much," she admitted. "But I do know Neal Makhav has something to do with the Penn case. And now he's gone missing."

Ross cocked his head. "Isn't he just hiding as part of the shadow test?"

"He asked me to get him in to see Aunt Tatiana. He's supposed to testify. Apparently he was there when Martin Penn was killed."

"What?"

Elana waved her hand impatiently. "Look, none of us know Neal well, or at all, really—which is the point. I think he's okay, but I think he's caught up in something and I mean to find out what it is. Do you want to help or what?"

They exchanged a glance, then Hemandar nodded. "There is something. We've been keeping it between ourselves—"

"What?"

"You know everybody spies on everybody else. But I'm a builder, I'm really good at countermeasures and, well, devices. And for a while now I've been tracking somebody or something that's spying on people, even past the bounds of what their treaties allow."

Elana blinked in surprise. "That's . . . that's serious. Do you know who it is?"

Hemandar and Ross exchanged another look. "We didn't want to get anybody expelled," said Ross.

"Tell me!"

Hemandar shrugged. "The devices all share subtle technological signatures. I've narrowed it down to one candidate:

"Jerome Bland-of-Tierra-del-Fuego has been spying on all of us."

• • •

Gavin watched the bots watch him.

This underground bunker wasn't a cell. There were three large vaulted chambers, well heated and lit, full of paper books, exercise equipment, and other diversions. He just wasn't interested in any of them. Gavin had always preferred to be out on the land; at the very least, he needed sunlight on his face. Was this what Bernie felt like, sitting uselessly in that abandoned cathedral?

He paced. He beat up on the exercise bots, and he ate so he'd have more energy for beating them up. But he hardly slept at all the first night. He was thinking about where his responsibilities lay.

Gavin hadn't been with Bernie when the accident happened. His brother was in the City. Simply, one Bernie had left on an ordinary morning, and another had come home that night in a swarm of human doctors and out-of-house bots. Gavin couldn't even get close to him, not for weeks. When he thought about that time, he often told himself that he'd never felt so helpless as he had then.

That was no longer true.

As he sat on the edge of a sumptuous bed that was really just a prison cot, Gavin could clearly picture the chill cavern outside the entrance to this apartment. He was imprisoned inside a lockstep fortress. The thing was, the place was familiar, in a deeply unsettling way. He *had* seen this fortress—or one like it—before.

The cold, blue light and vista of coffinlike cicada beds might have been the door through which he entered the memory, but he couldn't have opened that door without a key. And that key was this very feeling of helplessness.

He closed his eyes, and felt it again:

"Run, Gavin!"

He ran, his sister at his side, blinking, into light. Behind them a long shaft angled deep into the earth, its sides lit by electric light. The air rushing out of that shaft was icy cold. Ahead, a shimmering desert spread to the horizon under the gaze of a noonday sun.

"You can make it! Keep going! Hide if they come near."

He looked back, saw his parents' faces as they pushed him ahead. He saw his sister stumble, twist her ankle. Something was coming up the shaft behind them, something terrifying.

They had been friends! The family came over nearly every week, and Gavin had played with the boys, who were around his age. Then suddenly yesterday morning, Mom and Dad were warning him not to take their calls. Jubilee was ending, the monthly Big Sleep was coming, and Gavin wasn't able to say good-bye. He wasn't even allowed to sleep in his own bed, but tossed and turned in a strange metal-walled room that looked out on a creepy mist-shrouded cavern. And then woke too soon, and was told to run—

Gavin ran now, until everything became confused and all he had were the agonies of his own body and the fear in his mind. Next thing he knew, a man and a woman were standing over him in cold dawn light: Martin Chaffee and the woman Gavin would learn, briefly, to call Mother.

He had something to tell them, something about not trusting those old family friends. He struggled to remember—

But it was gone.

He sat there, still as Eli's statue, and the seconds ticked past. But what did it matter now? Even if he could have remembered everything, there was no one to tell.

• • •

Elana heard a faint noise and looked up. Her shadow was poking its head in the high window she had used to get into the library. "Stay!" she hissed at it.

Some casual conversation with Haixi Bang had taught her about motion detectors and thermal cameras. With some effort, she'd assigned a bit of her economy to discreetly produce countermeasures. Now she waved around a detector she'd had built. It registered six moving figures on this floor of the Doge's Palace, none of them human. Two were approaching on courses that would take them past her. She hid behind a pillar as one went by, her heart thudding painfully. Above, her shadow had not moved. That was a bit of a surprise.

When the sentry bot had receded, she sidled around the pillar and made for the stairs. It was easy if nerve-wracking to pad up them and find the door to the Archive's library. She used her sensor, which showed one slowly moving form within.

Elana crept down a darkened side corridor. There was

a second door here, which her casual daylight snooping had told her had an ancient-style keyhole. She bent to look through this and got a sliver of a view of the library. One light was on, and a nebulous shadow drifted across tall bookshelves. That could be anything. But who would be here this late, if not the Archive?

She slowly turned the doorknob and eased the heavy wooden slab open just a crack. There it was. The Archive wore an ornate red waistcoat and black trousers; its blue skin was the only indication that it wasn't human. Right now it was standing with an open book in its hand, its head tilted to one side as if contemplating something. It had probably memorized every book in here centuries ago, as well as millions of others. Why should it bother to reread something?

It lowered its head and raised the book. One hand held it, the other caressed the pages in a strangely fond gesture.

For a moment Elana felt acutely embarrassed, as though she'd walked in on an intensely private moment. The Archives were ancient AIs, of near-human intelligence. She shouldn't be surprised to discover that they loved what they did.

Since the bot was facing away from her, Elana gave herself a shake and pushed open the door, which let out a loud squeak.

The Archive turned just as Elana dove behind a red leather couch.

"Who's there?"

What was the password? For a second her mind went blank. Then she remembered the filename and safe word Eli had given Neal. She shouted them both quickly in a voice as unlike her own as she could.

She peeked over the back of the couch. The Archive had its back to her, its arms folded. "You wish this file?" it said. "I am allowed to provide you only with hard copy. Digitization is forbidden."

"That's fine." She felt ridiculous, crouched like this behind the furniture, but it was important that it not see her.

The Archive put down its book and walked to a printer in an alcove. It bent and seemed to cough at it. Seconds later, it drew out a large sheet of paper. "Place it on the coffee table and turn away," she said in her fake voice. When it did, she came around and snatched the paper, then retreated out the door. "Um, thanks!"

Downstairs, her shadow still waited at the window. "Be a dear and pull me up?" It didn't move. "Fine." Laboriously, she clambered up the rope and through the window. Outside was a nearly invisible platform attached to a long, similarly clear arm that angled upward. Hundreds of meters overhead, a faintly whirring drone waited to whisk her away. She climbed onto the platform, grinning at her shadow, which sat opposite, and canals and rooftops flickered underneath. "And that's how it's done!"

She could see her palace up ahead, its windows illuminating the street on one side and the dock on its other. She angled the drone to land on the darkened roof—mission accomplished!—then nearly capsized.

Someone was standing outside her palace door.

The figure was as still as a statue. She thought of Eli Makhav and his marble telepresence body, but as she circled warily above the square, she could see it wasn't that. This was a bot.

The drone dropped her a few meters away from it and arrowed up again in a dramatic whoosh of air. Her hair still settling from the downblast, she bowed slightly to Neal Makhav's shadow and said, "I thought you might show up. Come in."

The servants opened the door for her, and as they hurried about, her own shadow stepped into a corner as Neal's approached. "Can you speak?" she asked it. It didn't move. "Write?" No response. "Didn't think so. You can't find him, can you? Well, he isn't here, if that's why you came."

It didn't move.

"Fine, fine," she said, waggling the rolled-up document at it. "You're right, I'm looking for him, too; that's where I was just now." She went off the main hall to a dining table that could comfortably seat sixty. "Though how you lost him in the first place is beyond me," she added, jabbing a finger in the air as she slammed down the tube and unrolled it. "You'd think that you people, watching us like hawks all day and night, would have some idea . . ." She stared at the paper from the Archive.

There was no writing, just a photograph, dated to three thousand years ago. A family portrait with seven people in it, indistinct trees in the background. There was nothing odd or dramatic about it at all, until she squinted and recognized the faces she was looking at.

Elana cursed and sat down. "So that's it . . ."

She turned to Neal's shadow, saying, "Hey, are you thinking what I'm—" It was gone. From the front hall, she heard the main door slam.

She groaned. "Get after it!" she ordered. "No, wait, I'll go myself. I need a security team, not that light detail we had today, I mean serious firepower. Summon some family soldiers if you have to.

"Find me that shadow!"

• • •

There was a knock on Gavin's door.

Gavin started awake, cursing. "Wh-what time is it?"

He looked around, saw the glowing numbers on a clock: 2 a.m.

"Shit." He struggled to wake up as one of his jailer bots walked over to open the door. Gavin stood, flushed with adrenaline. One human figure and several robotic ones were silhouetted in the wintry light of the fortress cavern: Thomas Jagand-of-Karelia and his retinue of soldiers.

Gavin composed himself carefully and deliberately. "Come on in," he said drily. "It's not locked . . . from *that* side."

"I could come in," said Jagand. "Or you could come out, if you fancy a walk."

He grunted in surprise. But why not? He joined Jagand on a catwalk that stretched around the lower perimeter of the giant dome. The soldier bots (the same ones he'd seen with Jagand at Chaffee?) watched him attentively. "Pick a direction, then."

"You're not surprised to see me?"

"Who else would kidnap me on the eve of Bernie's trial?"

Jagand fell in beside him, the bots taking up positions behind. There was a long silence, punctuated only by the sound of their footsteps on the gridded catwalk. After only a few meters, the cold began to gnaw at Gavin, but he refused to show his discomfort. He was Neal Makhav, after all, notoriously stoic and arrogant.

"Family's very important to me," Jagand said suddenly. "Cutting yourself off from your father like that . . . it can't have been easy."

Gavin shrugged. "We never got along."

"But the chance to reconcile—if it were to come along . . . that would be a powerful force, I suspect." The auditor stopped, leaning on the railing and gazing out at the hibernation stacks.

Reluctantly, Gavin joined him. "I don't think that's going to happen."

"You haven't thanked me for helping you pass the shadow test," commented Jagand.

"Is that what this is? You're helping me?"

"Oh, I'm curious, too. Curious why you asked to see Bernard Penn's defender."

So he had been spying on the school. That really came as no surprise. Gavin shrugged, looked away.

"The chance to reconcile . . ." Jagand smile ruefully. "A man might try to make something right by helping a friend of his father's. By, say, changing his testimony to save the friend's son? Who might also be a friend?"

"I didn't actually see what happened."

"You've already said, in your statement, that you saw Bernie run from a burning house before my airships set down. When I arrived, Bernard Penn was raving about a secret brother and swore you killed him. Of course, there was no such person, was there?"

Gavin didn't answer.

"If Bernie had been a friend of yours, or if you had . . . other reasons, I can see how the official version of things might make you uncomfortable." Jagand smiled in a grandfatherly way. "The trial is going to find Bernard Penn guilty and sentence him to exile in the lockstep. It's a shame, really, and you might be tempted to give some other account of things, which might implicate someone else in Martin Penn's death.

"You might, for instance, think that saving Bernard requires that you implicate me. But you see, *I've* given no statement yet; I've been using my position as an auditor to defer doing that. So when I take the stand tomorrow I can easily say that your aircar was already on the ground and empty when I arrived. And guess what? New evidence suggests it had been there for some time. I'll produce a set of tracks parallel to Bernie's—a new discovery proving that you were in the house with him when Martin was killed. After all, I control the investigation. It'll be a simple matter to have you both convicted as coconspirators."

Gavin clenched his fists and would have launched himself at the auditor if the soldier bots hadn't had their weapons trained on him. He waited until he could speak without his voice shaking, then said, "You're not all-powerful. In fact, for all your posturing, you're in just as precarious a position as I am. I mean, if the other senior auditors were part of your conspiracy, then you'd be able to control our shadows. You wouldn't have had to hide me from mine. You don't actually control very much here in Venice, do you?"

That hit home. Jagand looked away for a few moments. "As I said," he said slowly, "family is very important to me. I'd do anything for my family; it's all that we really have in the end, isn't it?" The auditor looked Gavin over, frowning as if inspecting a defective bot. "I really had hoped for a better reaction from you. It would be so much easier if you stood up tomorrow and told the story we agreed on. But I see now that you can't be trusted to do that."

Gavin stepped back. "What are you—"

"Oh, I'm not going to kill you. You should thank me. After all, I've already made you disappear off the face of the Earth. Nothing would be easier than erasing you permanently. But that might cause more suspicion than it's worth. No." Jagand turned away. "All I have to do is wait a few days, then let your shadow find you somewhere unlikely but plausible, somewhere a Makhav would be likely to go to ground. You'll join Bernard Penn in lockstep exile, and that will be the end of it."

Gavin took another step back, and another. There must be some way out of this trap. He had fragmentary memories of how these fortresses were laid out, and he'd escaped from one before. He just couldn't remember how.

As he desperately scanned the cold hibernation racks below the gallery, something down there moved.

Jagand's soldier bots had closed in on him again. "Take him back to his quarters and make sure he's comfortable," said the auditor. "It's important he's undamaged when we 'track him down' in a week or so."

Gavin glanced at the hibernation stacks again; nothing was moving. Still, he was sure of what he'd seen. So he swore, he yelled, and he twisted to escape the arms of the soldier bots. He kicked up as much of a fuss as he could and was rewarded as Jagand and his forces kept their attention on him—

—and not on what approached quietly and steadily across the lockstep fortress's floor.

• • •

The last of the bots slammed the door as Elana took a quick look around the empty apartment she'd broken into. An ancient upright piano stood in the corner, and she dove behind it as a sword pierced the door behind her with a sharp *bang.*

"Keep 'em out!" She crouched there, her own blade half raised, and watched silhouetted figures kick the door open. Metal flashed in the early morning light to the sound of gnashing steel.

In seconds it was all over. The attackers had fallen. Her four remaining security bots sheathed their swords and turned to her for instruction. She stood shakily. "Come on."

This was some lockstepper's Venetian home, a nice place with a view of the Campo San Julian. Dust lay thick on white plastic-wrapped furniture and sculptures, incongruous as giant larvae in these ancient chambers. By treaty, only some of Venice's buildings could be used by the Million, and this wasn't one of them. Elana's very presence here was a crime.

She had bigger things to worry about. Five minutes ago, she'd had seventeen bots. Now she had four. They were being stabbed, crushed, torn to pieces—mostly at the city's inevitable choke points, the canal bridges she had to cross to reach her goal. The fight had been silent so far, and she knew if she broke that silence with any cry for help—acoustic or electronic—the gloves would come off. They'd take the building down around her if they had to, explain it away later. Her only advantage was that her pursuers wanted to keep this hunt quiet.

She couldn't leave the same way she'd come in. They would be waiting. Forcing herself to breathe deliberately and slowly, she moved to the apartment's inner door.

This building, like many in Venice, was built around a central courtyard. Her feet made grinding sounds on ancient fallen plaster; there was no way to be quiet. Easing the door open, she listened for approaching footsteps. If she couldn't be silent, neither could the assassins. In the momentary safety that the silence implied, she tightened the makeshift bandage she'd knotted around her wrist. A sword had slipped past her parry and given her that gash an hour ago.

It must be eight o'clock; the silver sky of dawn was giving way to blue. Hard to believe it had been only a couple of hours since one of her bots had run up to her, saying, "Ma'am, we've found Neal Makhav's shadow."

"Where?" She'd been patrolling far and wide but was starting to think the thing had left Venice entirely.

"One of us spotted it moving around the base of a lockstep fortress venting stack near the Fondamento Nuovo," said the bot. "When we reached the area, it had disappeared."

She hadn't believed it at first. Vanished . . . by a venting stack? Lockstep fortresses were the most heavily guarded facilities on the planet. There was no getting into one, though every few years some jackass tried. They were generally never seen again.

Then again, lockstep auditors emerged from them now and then, to check up on the Million. It was easy for them to come and go. What if one had friends among the Million's auditors?

"Show me that stack."

She raced through the courtyard to a door on its opposite side. She saw movement in the corridor, so she went left. "Break that window!" Her bots helped her through the shattered portal into another dark, empty apartment. Behind her she heard the thudding of bots' feet entering the courtyard. She'd zigged, they were zagging. All she had to do was keep this up across another couple of streets and plazas.

Elana and her team had reached the venting stack at 3 a.m. The floodlights and colored washes that normally painted the airships' undersides were muted now. She could see the Milky Way spangled behind them. The stack itself, an incongruous tall white cylinder, thrust up from the end of an ancient, crumbling wharf. The only sound was the slapping of water against its sides and, somewhere distant, the hollow knocking of a gondola against its mooring.

Elana was halfway down the wharf when a black oval suddenly appeared in the side of the stack. Two human figures tumbled out of it. One helped the other to his feet and they began to run—staggering to a halt as they saw Elana's team.

"Neal?"

"Elana? What are you doing here?"

"I'm looking for you. You could be a little grateful."

The oval entrance in the stack had disappeared, but now it was back, and vomiting more people. Bots, she realized. "Who're those—"

"Run! Just run!" He pelted past her, his shadow hard on his heels. The bots pouring out of the stack carried guns, knives, nets, and other unidentifiable but threatening things. Elana followed Neal and heard the first of her security detail go into the water behind her.

She caught up to Neal, and he flashed her a quick smile. "We have to get into the city! They won't risk waking anybody with gunfire."

"Where were you? What happened?"

"Jagand. Karelia. Wants to keep me from testifying. Held me in the lockstep fortress."

She'd gotten just a bit more out of him. He'd been sitting in his prison when his shadow walked in. For some reason Neal had been expecting that—"Locked from the inside, not the outside!" he'd said with a laugh—and he'd grabbed its arm and fled. "Knew they wouldn't fire if we used the hibernation stacks as cover—killing locksteppers is the ultimate treaty violation—so we played hide-and-seek across the cavern and made it here."

On shore now, both ducked as two of Elana's bots got in the way of projectiles. They staggered, bullets whined overhead, and on the wharf a high-speed sword fight sent limbs and heads tumbling.

"I'll hold them off, you make for the courthouse," she said. "Take a small squad—now, go!"

In hindsight, she should have brought flying equipment. Radio jammers had cut off her team from signaling the aerostat and the rest of the city, and in seconds she and Neal were separated, fleeing down different alleys with an auditor's private army behind them.

Now one of her bots cracked the lock on an outside apartment and they quickly moved through that to its front windows. Enemies were everywhere, but there was also good cover outside—low walls, ornamental trees, statuary. Past the next intersection, the towers of the Doge's Palace were catching flame colors from the rising sun.

And there, at last, were people—real people, not fakes—strolling across the broad plaza in the direction of the courthouse.

Neal suddenly sprinted out of a darkened doorway, followed by his shadow. As one, the bots that had been prowling outside Elana's apartment building converged on them.

"Now!" She kicked a bot and it dove through the window into the street. Screaming an incoherent battle cry and with her sword held high, she followed. With her four guards flanking her, she ran straight at the enemy.

It was time for saber moves. She cut and stabbed, dodged a riposte, kicked one attacker into another, and beheaded a third. Two of her own went down as she did this. "Take them out!" she cried to the last two. She pointed at three foes that had nearly caught up to Neal. "I'll keep these back!"

She turned, and suddenly a new squad of black-garbed bots was moving to flank her from the left. And leading them—

"Jerome? You traitor!"

The scarred heir of Tierra del Fuego didn't bother to reply. Arrogantly ignoring his watching shadow, he lowered his sword and pointed it at Elana. His bots drew as one and marched toward her.

"Coward!" she screamed at him. "Face me yourself!" It was obvious Bland knew her too well to do that. Cursing, Elana ducked around the brawl her own bots were in and ran for Neal.

He was in the Piazza San Marco, alone, with six pursuers on his tail. They were going to catch him, and she was too far away—

Echoing over the piazza came the sound of a horn, sonorous, powerful, and low. And out of an archway up ahead, a mob of swearing, shouting Rosses appeared. Cutting off Neal's pursuers, they ran at Jagand's bots, howling and waving their sabers.

The horn sounded again, and something else clogged the archway—a giant mechanical elephant. It raised its trunk, letting loose a third blast, and charged.

Neal laughed and ran under the elephant's legs. Several of the people on the courthouse footbridge turned to look.

Jagand's bots stopped so suddenly that Elana ran into one of them. She raised her blade to cut it down, but it was turning away. They all were, even Jerome Bland's, even as he stood cursing, hopping up and down and ordering them to keep going.

Thomas Jagand-of-Karelia couldn't let his bots be seen gutting one of the Hundred in the street. They couldn't be seen tackling and carting off today's star witness. Neal was safe; so was she.

She walked up to him as a protective cordon of Rosses ringed them and Jerome ran after his departing squad. She and Neal were both panting too much to speak. All she could do was mutely hold out the rolled-up—and now crumpled—picture from the archive. Gavin took it, puzzled.

"Proof," she said, "of something bigger than just—" Suddenly dizzy and weak, she sat down on the cobblestones. As Karelia's soldiers gathered up the fallen combatants—carting away the evidence—both Gavin and her shadow knelt next to her.

"Elana!" Gavin was shaking her.

"She doesn't appear to be badly injured, sir," said one of her two remaining bots. "I believe this is exhaustion. We've reestablished communications with the Devries aerostat, and they have ordered us to bring her home to be treated. She will receive the best care."

"No," she muttered. "I have to see this through. I want to see you tell . . ." She couldn't stop herself leaning over farther and onto the cobbles. She vaguely felt Neal's hand land on her shoulder.

"Thanks," he said. "I know what to do now."

• • •

Bots in Makhav livery were waiting for Gavin at the top of the courthouse steps. He shied away, then heard a familiar laugh. "You can trust these ones, Son."

Eli Makhav stepped out from behind a pillar. "Your servants were either disassembled or locked up when I got to town. Been looking for you. Come this way." Numb, Gavin followed him to a small iron door off the main entrance to the courthouse. Only when he was inside with the door closed and locked did he slump against the pale green guardhouse wall and let out a heavy sigh of relief.

He reached out to clasp his shadow by the shoulder. "Thanks."

Eli looked amused. "You had other help, too. What just happened?"

While Makhav house bots wiped the sweat off his face, brought out fresh clothes, and made his hair decent, Gavin described his imprisonment and the running battle to escape. "I wouldn't be here if it weren't for Elana."

Eli nodded. "Smart of her to tail your shadow. Think she'll be all right?"

"She'd better be." Gavin straightened, setting aside his exhaustion. Now that he was dressed again, one of the bots handed back the crumpled tube of paper Elana had given him; he tucked it into his belt. "Am I still able to testify?"

"They can't stop you now," said another familiar voice. It was Destiny Kolwezi, leaning in an inner doorway. She usually dressed in auditor's blacks, but the belts and bulky pouches hanging from her waist weren't standard classroom attire. Gavin recognized sensors, communications devices, and a couple of unobtrusive weapons.

"The only question," she said, "is what are you going to tell the court?"

"The truth," said Gavin. He glanced at Eli. "She knows?"

Makhav nodded.

"I'll tell them that I'm Bernie's brother. That Thomas

Jagand-of-Karelia killed my father and that I took Neal Makhav's place. I'll back Bernie up."

Eli nodded slowly. "And when they ask me how I failed to notice that you weren't my nephew, what do you expect me to say?"

Gavin narrowed his eyes. "Deny me. Whatever you have to do, I don't—" But Eli was shaking his head. "You selfish bastard!"

"It's not that," said Eli. "There's more at stake here than your own honor."

"This isn't about honor! It's about Bernie's life!"

"Before this gets ugly," said Kolwezi, interposing herself between them, "I think there's something you need to see."

Much as he wanted to punch Eli's smug face, Gavin held back. With a growl, he let Kolwezi lead them through the courthouse's labyrinth of administrative chambers. Whatever she had in mind, he knew his next destination: Councilor Tatiana Devries-of-Balashikha's office. He had to tell her what he knew, let her add his testimony to the defense's argument.

Kolwezi stopped at a side-stage window that looked out over the courtroom. The gallery was filling with spectators. "Disgusting," said Gavin. This was Bernie's ultimate nightmare: being put on public display like some captured monster. He shuddered and started to turn away, but Kolwezi said, "Second level, center gallery. Those people. Who are they?"

Gavin looked up—and stumbled back. "Hell!"

Eli and Destiny exchanged a glance. "You recognize them?" she asked.

He couldn't speak, just stared at Kolwezi and Makhav in turn. Eli sighed heavily and held out a hand to one of his retinue. "Photo, please." One handed him a rectangle of printed paper, and he in turn passed it to Gavin. "Look familiar?"

Gavin held the thing away from him, as if it were on fire. "They were our friends!"

Eli nodded. "Your family's friends. In the lockstep.

"But something happened, didn't it? Your parents found out about a plan, or a plot. Maybe they overheard accidentally, were just in the wrong place at the wrong time. And then the plotters had to shut you up."

Gavin reluctantly moved back to the window. "Who are they pretending to be?"

"Members of the Vera clan, of Almaty. They've been vouched for, genealogies produced, everything confirmed. They're as real a pack of Veras as you are a Makhav."

Gavin twisted his shaking hands together, trying to extinguish old flames of memory. "But why are they here? Why now?"

Destiny's look was pitying. "To take the Chaffee lands when Bernie's gone."

They were both watching Gavin in that way the people at Bernie's party had watched him. Waiting for the explosion. Somehow, recognizing that flipped everything around for Gavin. He pictured himself hovering over everything he'd done in the past months, looking down at himself in the same way. He'd been waiting to explode; he'd planned it. He'd even known the date and the venue: today, here.

He laughed and shook his head. "Oh."

If anything, Eli and Destiny looked even more alarmed. "Let me guess," Gavin went on. "If I were to trace Thomas Jagand's family tree way, way back, I'd find the Veras in it, wouldn't I? They're his ancestors."

Destiny nodded. "How'd you know?"

"Something he said. So this is what it was all about, all along. Bringing his family from the lockstep into real time. They—we—weren't poor in the lockstep, but we weren't anybody in particular, I remember that. We were just people, I'm sure that was true for them there, too. But here . . . Here, they'd be the Million."

The reason for the death of his parents and sister, and ultimately for Martin's murder and Bernie's disgrace—it was all so ordinary. Banal, almost a letdown. Gavin found that where he expected anger, he felt nothing at all.

"Well," he said, "let's take them down."

"Or," said Eli, in what was for him an almost pleading tone of voice, "let's not."

It had never occurred to Gavin that Eli's role might be to clean up after Karelia's messes. "How did I miss it?" he said, wondering at his own stupidity.

"It's not what you think," said Eli.

"Get out of my way."

"Gavin, there's more you need to know—"

He was determined not to listen, but Destiny Kolwezi's words were so unexpected he stopped with his hand on the doorjamb.

"You're not the first!"

He didn't want to turn, or say, "What do you mean?" Shoulders slumped, he waited.

Destiny said, "We—Eli and I—we don't think this was just a conspiracy. We think it might be a . . ."

"A policy," said Eli.

"Think of it!" Destiny reached out, stopped short of grabbing Gavin's arm. "If some family of the Million were to die out every century or so, and be replaced by extra members of some other, obscure clan . . . who would even notice? It would happen so seldom, once in a lifetime as far as we'd be concerned. But on the lockstep side, if those 'extra clan members' were really coming from there, they'd be sending them into our world *every two or three months*!"

"You asked . . ." Gavin shook his head. "In class once, you asked why we spoke the same language as the lock-steppers. Why our names are so similar, and our culture. We were always taught it's because they're always there, and we meet them again every thirty years. You're saying there's another reason."

She nodded. "It's not because they visit us. It's because they *are* us."

Gavin pictured a slow overturn of the Million's population, managed century by century by the lockstep, as a gardener manages his oblivious flowers. "You're saying joining the Million is a reward for good service or something? A . . . a retirement plan? And all you have to do is make sure that one or another of our families is always reduced to two or three people, easy to cull and replace . . ."

Destiny nodded. "They would have to bribe or threaten some of us to sponsor the replacements. Play on the vanity of people like Thomas Jagand. And who better to work through than the auditors?"

Gavin thought for a while. "Thank you for telling me this."

"You see, we don't know how far the conspiracy goes," said Eli. "Or what the consequences might be if we exposed it. Who's involved, how powerful they are—"

"I get it, I do. Thanks. It doesn't change anything." He turned away again.

He heard Eli shouting, railing at Destiny to stop him, and scuffling as she apparently held him back. Gavin didn't care. He left them standing backstage and threaded his way to Councilor Devries's chamber. His mind, once again, was blank.

It was when he was outside Tatiana's door, about to announce himself to the bot guarding it, that something happened to break the bubble of numbness. As he shifted and opened his mouth to speak, Gavin's hand brushed his belt and something crackled dully. He blinked, looked down, and remembered the rolled-up paper Elana had passed to him. He'd meant to open it immediately, but Eli and Destiny had distracted him.

He stared, frowning, at the ancient photo of the Veras. Then he turned away from Tatiana Devries's door.

• • •

Hundreds of faces, every eye turned toward the witness box. A few months ago, being in such a position would have been terrifying. Now Gavin ignored all but a few of them:

Eli and Destiny, seated uncomfortably in the first gallery.

The Veras, strange mirror images of people he'd known when he was very young. Unchanged by time, their expressions blank as they pretended not to notice him noticing them.

Thomas Jagand-of-Karelia, on the main floor near a back exit. He looked very nervous. Gavin almost smiled.

In the very top gallery, near the back, a pale Elana Devries-of-Balashikha was being helped into a seat by Ross and Hemandar. Now Gavin did smile.

And there, at last, was Bernie, sitting with Tatiana Devries. His expression was hopeful as he met Gavin's eye. Gavin lost the smile.

The auditors' prosecutor rose, approached, and began the formalities. He asked Gavin his name. "Neal Makhav-of-Winter-Park." He asked how Neal knew the Chaffees, and whether he had any kind of friendship with Bernard Penn-of-Chaffee. Neal admitted to a passing acquaintance.

These preliminaries dragged on, and Gavin began to wake to where he was and what he was about to say. His pulse was beginning to speed up, he could feel sweat on his forehead, and the prosecutor was starting to repeat his questions as Gavin's attention faltered. He glanced up at Elana, but that didn't help. She was leaning forward, hands clutching the back of the bench below her.

Somehow, she had gotten hold of the same photo of

the Veras as Eli had. That meant she knew some of it, at least, if not all. Without his willing it, she had been thrust into the center of a storm, where Eli Makhav and Destiny Kolwezi had freely chosen to be.

It wasn't right. She would be a target now. If she'd told Tatiana what she knew, the whole Devries clan might be in danger.

The prosecutor cleared his throat. "Can you tell me what you saw as you approached the Chaffee estate?"

This was the question Gavin had been anticipating since he landed in Venice. He had rehearsed his next words many times, mostly as he lay unsleeping in a Makhav bed, in the place Eli deigned to keep for him. All this time, he'd known what he would say.

He couldn't help looking at Bernie as he abandoned that speech. "The . . . house was on fire. I could see that from the air. I wasn't intending to land, I was following the auditors because I'd decided to join up if I could. What I saw was"—he took a deep breath—"the auditors were circling. They hadn't landed yet. I saw no gunfire or sign that they had attacked in any way. The fire . . . it was inside, the windows weren't broken. And then Bernie—Bernard Penn—came running out."

As Gavin spoke these words, his brother's eyes widened, and all the color drained from his face. Gavin couldn't look away, even as the prosecutor asked for more details and he supplied them. As he lied about confronting Bernie and hearing him rave about an imaginary sibling, he mentally urged his brother to vault over the table, to cry foul, to declare Gavin to be an impostor. *Something,* anything. But Bernie just sat there, his shocked expression slowly sagging into one of acceptance and resignation. He thought he knew the choice Gavin had made. He thought he understood it—and that hurt most of all.

Gavin didn't remember the rest of his testimony, afterward. He knew Tatiana Devries had cross-examined him, but he had no idea what they said to each other. The courtroom audience had faded, as had the judge and the rest of the officials. Gavin sat alone, under Bernie's pitying gaze.

When he returned to his seat, he did notice Thomas Jagand-of-Karelia nodding in guarded approval. Everything else was a blur.

And when it was all over, they found Bernie guilty, and he was taken away. The prosecutors shook hands as they rose, and everywhere chairs slid back, people gabbled energetic nonsense at one another, pages ran back and forth, and retinues laid red carpets for their masters as the Million dismissed today's entertainment. They had other things to do.

Gavin remained seated, his hands clasped together on

the tabletop, until Elana appeared and gently lifted him to his feet.

• • •

The spires of a fairy castle broke through the intricately scrolled shell of the Devries aerostat. One tower was rounded by windows whose fretwork was carved into the shapes of branches. Stained-glass leaves in red, gold, and green interrupted the clear panes here and there. Far below, the Mediterranean Sea was a pan of silver speckled with bright highlights. All of this was nearly beautiful enough that Elana could ignore the aircraft, drones, and hoverbots of the Devries military clouding around the aerostat like bees around a threatened hive.

Tatiana Devries sat in a tall chair under one of the windows, her hands steepled under her chin. To her left was Eli Makhav and to her right, Destiny Kolwezi. Elana couldn't sit still; she was prowling angrily in front of them. Her shadow wasn't with her, and that felt odd. It stood just outside the door, forcibly detained by Devries house bots.

"I do *not* understand!" Elana glared at Makhav, who seemed amused by the fact that he couldn't intimidate her. "Jagand kidnapped Neal. We barely escaped with our lives! Neal was going to tell the court that the Veras are visitors and that Jagand helped them grab the Chaffee lands. He was going to destroy Jagand. And he didn't do it. He toed the line. Why?"

Makhav shrugged. "You'll have to ask him when you find him. He's seeing Bernie off to the underworld as we speak."

"Assuming he didn't have a change of heart and say something there," said Kolwezi. She smiled. "Or challenged Jagand to a duel. I can't believe Neal's going through with it, attending the exile ceremony in person."

"He has things to tell Bern," said Eli. "It can't be easy, but if he just lets him go . . ."

Elana stopped pacing. "Could you get any more coy? What's going on here?"

"It's not for us to say," Makhav said imperturbably. "Besides, you know most of it."

"That the Veras are from the lockstep? That they conspired with Jagand to replace the Penns as stewards of Chaffee? Sure. But why haven't you told the other auditors? Why didn't Neal tell the court he'd been imprisoned and threatened by Jagand?" Elana put her fists on her hips and committed herself to saying what she'd suspected all along. "All of the auditors are in on it!"

"Well, I'm not," Destiny said mildly. "Nor anyone in the school. But the others . . . maybe. We don't know. That's why Neal made the right decision. He could have exposed Jagand, but that would have alerted the rest of them."

"But it could have led to an investigation! We could have ferreted them all out!"

"Maybe." Eli Makhav sighed. "And maybe we would have eliminated the problem, on our side, for an entire generation. Or two, or a century. That would be just a season from the lockstep's point of view. They can wait a few Jubilees before starting the operation again. No, it's not enough to eliminate the conspiracy on our side. We have to kill it in the lockstep as well. And we won't have a chance to do that for two years."

Destiny nodded. "That's how long we have to figure all of this out." In two years the lockstep fortresses would open, spilling billions of people onto the planet. It was true that the great estates of the Million would be overrun with tourists. But it was equally true that, according to ancient custom and the originating treaties, the Million would be free to move among the locksteppers as citizens. Wealthy, powerful, and united. During that one month, they would wield real power. They just had to know how to use it.

Finally feeling tired, Elana sat down. "Do you suppose all this has happened before?" she asked. "The replacements, the Million finding out . . . Do you suppose they replace all of us at once, every now and then? Over all these thousands of years . . . How would we know?"

Makhav nodded. "Destiny and I have had that nightmare, too. That's why Neal was right to do what he did. What if the rest of us find out about the Veras? What happens in two years? We might confront the locksteppers when they wake, only to have it that when they go back to sleep, none of us are here any longer. A new Million might have taken our place."

It violated all treaties. Elana had been raised to think of the ancient compact between the lockstep and the Million as sacred, and as constant as the sun and moon. "While they sleep, we have the power," she said, but her heart was in her throat. Asleep, the lockstep was vulnerable, but surely the vast majority of its people were innocent. To attack them in their helplessness would be evil, plain and simple.

"Let Eli and me worry about the lockstep," said Destiny. Indicating Tatiana, she added, "Your aunt is a part of this now. We'll figure out what the Million's options are. It may well be that this has happened before, but if so, the proof will be in the libraries, or the genealogies, or the ruins outside the museum cities. The locksteppers aren't the only ones able to send messages into the deep future, and it may well be that our ancestors foresaw this and left clues for us. We'll look into that. Meanwhile, you and Neal have a different task. If you're able to become auditors, you must explore the problem from the inside. If not . . . I hate to admit the scale of the sacrifices that might be necessary. To get to the bottom of it, you might someday be called on to enter lockstep time. We have to face the fact that our investigation might last far longer than the lives of any of us in this room. You had better be prepared to leave all of us behind, if it should come to that."

Stunned, Elana sat back. For a long time, nobody spoke. Then, glancing up, Elana saw Tatiana watching her.

She squared her shoulders, but Destiny's words were still ringing inside her head. Right now she wanted nothing more than to run to Katharine, be enfolded in the sympathy and genuine love of her older sister. Yet Katharine didn't know what was happening, and couldn't know.

"What is it?" Tatiana asked suddenly.

Elana grimaced. "I thought I was being so brave, joining the auditors to weed out corruption. I had this great career path in mind, me the reformer, upholding the Devries standard . . . retiring to great acclaim and the respect of the Hundred. That's not going to happen now, is it?"

Their silence was sufficient answer.

• • •

Once, he had run to his brother past a hundred fakes and statues, and flung open the doors to the Chaffee ballroom knowing what his exposure would cost. Now Gavin walked aisles lined with a different sort of statue. The sleeping locksteppers were invisible beneath the frosted lids of their cicada beds, but he felt their presence. It was like he'd thrown open the doors only to find the dancers frozen in midstep. All unaware of him.

He didn't need the auditors' bots to guide him, for the only light came from up ahead, where the aisles converged. In an open space there, Bernie was sitting on the edge of an ordinary-looking bed, eyes downcast. An arc of human figures was half-visible in the darkness behind him.

There were auditors from the Million here, and others from the lockstep wakened specifically to authorize Bernie's passage from real time to their half-world. The uniforms, lined faces, and stiff bearing of those present should have intimidated him. When Thomas Jagand saw Gavin, he started visibly, then scowled. But Neal Makhav knew Bernie; he had a perfect right to be here.

"I'd like to say good-bye to my friend," he said loudly as he stepped into the space between the auditors and the bed. "Alone."

Jagand licked his lips, his eyes darting around. But the senior auditors nodded gravely and stepped back into the shadows. Reluctantly, Jagand followed.

There would be some terrible reckoning, someday; whether Jagand would catch Gavin first, or he would take the auditor down, remained to be seen.

As Gavin stopped a few feet away, Bernie looked him up and down. Gavin had hoped to see him putting on a brave face. He'd imagined Bernie joking at the end. Really, he just looked scared. "Why'd you come?" he asked.

Gavin flinched. "I tried. Bern, it was all I did."

"I know." Bernie shrugged. "I know what it came down to. Either me down here alone, or both of us. You chose right."

"That's not it!" This was what Gavin had been afraid of. "I didn't run out on you, Bernie. If it were up to me, I'd be right here with you. But it wouldn't have done any good."

Bernie clutched the edge of the bed, visibly struggling to control himself. "But Jagand, he's still—" Muscles rippled in his arms; he looked down, shaking his head.

"We could have brought him down, yes." Gavin stepped close, taking Bernie by the shoulders, trying to make him meet his eye. "But we'd have missed his masters."

Bernie looked up, seeming to forget his anger. Gavin had seen this melting away of his fury many times, and he stepped back in relief. He nodded. "Do you want me to take the pawn, or the king?"

"Both." Bernie glared into the darkness where Jagand stood. He turned his attention to Gavin, and there was the old Bernard Chaffee, visibly thinking things through. "There's more to it, then?" Gavin nodded. Bernie chewed on that for a while, then nodded thoughtfully. "See you in two years?"

Gavin couldn't stop the tears anymore. Bernie stepped forward and they hugged. As Bernie broke away, he said, "Make sure those Vera bastards take proper care of our land."

"I will." Gavin hesitated, then said, "Bernie? I . . . always wanted to ask you. Were you there, that day? When Dad found me?"

Bernie sat back down on the bed. "Ah. Yeah, yeah I was."

"Was there . . . was there anybody else? I don't mean, necessarily, alive . . ."

Bernie was shaking his head. "Just one little boy in lockstep clothes, wandering alone in the desert. We didn't have to talk about it, Dad and Mom and me. We just brought you home."

Gavin took a ragged breath. "Okay." He turned to go,

then said, "Two years."

"Two years," Bernie agreed, and he took his feet off the floor and Gavin walked past the auditors and the hibernation bots, back into the lightless maze of the lockstep fortress.

• • •

"Shadows! Rise!"

Elana's silent companion stood. All across the assembly hall, the other students' shadows were doing the same. She glanced down the row, saw Hemandar and Ross both looking nervous. Neal Makhav didn't seem to notice as the dark figure that had accompanied him everywhere these past months finally left his side.

He had begun to rouse out of his numb indifference a little in recent days. Just enough to complete his classes, write the tests. He seemed good at going through the motions.

Though they were supposedly identical, it was easy for Elana to pick out her own shadow as the auditors' devices lined up on stage behind Dean Tuyuc-of-Cuzco. Once you got to know them, you felt the nearly indefinable sense of individuality they carried. They weren't like house bots, or even like the military AIs that the auditors were allowed to use. Their very existence suggested a dimension of possible relationships with the Million's technology that Elana had never thought of before coming to this school. They were disturbing; they were supposed to be.

"Each of you has had a chance to evade your shadow, and to find it as it tried to evade you," said the dean. "By itself, how well you did doesn't decide whether you'll pass this term. But it could make or break a narrow decision.

"I'm going to call each of you by name, in turn, and your shadow will step forward and deliver its verdict. Pass or fail." She began to call out names.

Elana turned to Neal. "They *can* talk!" The first one had just said, *"Fail!"* Down in front, Jerome Bland-of-Tierra-del-Fuego was cursing under his breath.

Neal shrugged. "It's not like we don't know what ours are going to say. After what we got up to this term . . ."

"Thanks. I've been trying to be optimistic!"

"Ssh!" Ross impatiently flapped a hand at them.

The names rolled out, one by one, each shadow stepping forward, speaking one word, and moving back. Elana watched them, twisting her hands together. It seemed to be taking forever.

"Ross Donegal-of-Finn!"

"Pass!"

Ross nodded as if it had been a foregone conclusion.

Time passed. Then: "Hemandar Satna-of-Delhi."

"Fail!"

Hemandar winced, then waggled his head from side to side. "My marks are good. I'll try again."

"Elana Devries-of-Balashikha!"

"Pass!"

"Wha—?" She looked at Neal, who had suddenly taken an interest in the proceedings.

"Neal Makhav-of-Winter-Park."

"Pass!"

His shadow made way for the next one; Elana suddenly realized that hers was no longer visible. After giving their verdict, the bots were leaving the stage. Suddenly it seemed strange, and somehow wrong, that she would never see it again.

Students who'd passed or failed were rising and leaving the chamber. Through the burgeoning crowd Elana spotted a bot in Devries livery approaching. It bowed as she met it at the end of the aisle, and said, "Your aunt Tatiana has requested your presence, ma'am. Yourself, and Neal Makhav."

She turned to find him already behind her. Elana gave a deep, slightly shaky sigh. "First step accomplished. We'll be auditors."

He nodded, obviously surprised by the test result. Then again, their shadows couldn't fault them for being sneaky—and maybe that had been the point of the test all along.

"What's our next step?" he asked.

She smiled.

"Come with me, and we'll figure it out."

About the Author

KARL SCHROEDER has authored ten novels, including the Aurora Award–winning *Lockstep,* which is set in the same universe as *The Million,* and the Virga series. He is a member of the Association of Professional Futurists, and in 2018 was awarded the Netexplo Talent of the Year Award for blockchain innovation. When not writing, he consults and speaks on the potential impact of emerging technologies on humanity and natural systems. Karl lives in Toronto, Ontario, with his wife and daughter.

www.kschroeder.com

TOR·COM

Science fiction. Fantasy. The universe.

And related subjects.

*

More than just a publisher's website, *Tor.com* is a venue for **original fiction, comics,** and **discussion** of the entire field of SF and fantasy, in all media and from all sources. Visit our site today—and join the conversation yourself.